THE DRAGON'S BIDDER

Tahoe Dragon Mates #3

JESSIE DONOVAN

Mythical Lake Press, LLC

This book is a work of fiction. Names, characters, places, and incidents are either the product of the writer's imagination or are used fictitiously, and any resemblance to actual persons, living or dead, business establishments, events, or locales is entirely coincidental.

Want to stay up to date on releases? Please join my newsletter by clicking here to sign-up.

Books in this series:

Tahoe Dragon Mates

The Dragon's Choice (TDM #1)
The Dragon's Need (TDM #2)
The Dragon's Bidder / (TDM #3)
The Dragon's Charge / Brad & Tasha (TDM #4 / Nov 12, 2020)
The Dragon's Weakness / David & Tiffany (TDM #5 / Jan 14, 2021)

The Dragon's Bidder Synopsis

In exchange for favors to help his clan, PineRock's dragon leader Wes Dalton agrees to participate in a charity auction. After all, one evening dining or dancing with one lucky bidder shouldn't be too hard to endure. Then he notices the true mate he can never have in the audience—Ashley Swift. When she wins him for the night, the battle begins between what his dragon half wants and what his human half tries to deny.

Ashley Swift worked her way up the ranks of the American Department of Dragon Affairs and knows the ins and outs of dragon-shifters in her area. And while it's against the rules and she knows it, Ashley is drawn to PineRock's clan leader. They've danced around each other for years, but Ashley has finally found a way to spend an evening with Wes—a charity auction. Nothing in the rules prevents her from bidding, and she wins. One night is all she needs to get him out of her system, or so she tries to tell herself.

As the pair dance around their undeniable attraction to one another, more than Ashley's job or Wes's position is at stake. They stumble upon unrest brewing in Reno, and it's up to them to protect the clan. Only then can they think of a way to skirt the rules and be together.

NOTE: This is a quick, steamy standalone story about fated mates and sexy dragon-shifters near Lake Tahoe in the USA. You don't have to read all my other dragon books to enjoy this one!

Chapter One

Wes Dalton barely resisted tearing off his stupid, confining blazer, and reminded himself of why he was standing backstage inside a human casino in Reno, Nevada dressed to the nines.

He owed Ashley Swift and the American Department of Dragon Affairs—ADDA—more than one favor. And to repay it, he'd agreed to be one of the dragon males auctioned off for the night, the proceeds going to charity.

In other words, he'd have to put aside his usual dominance and tendency to take charge like he did as clan leader and follow the whims of some stranger.

Even with rules in place, Wes wasn't looking forward to it.

His inner dragon—his other half and the second personality inside his head—snorted. *Don't act like it's the worst thing in the world. After all, the rules mean we don't have to kiss or fuck anyone.*

True, but some human females obsessed with dragon-shifters might try to break those rules and that wasn't something he wanted to deal with. *Regardless, I don't like being away from PineRock even if it's for just an evening.*

A lot had happened over the last nine months back on his clan, ever since one human and then another had come to live with his people. Not only had a mutiny been brewing among a handful of his clan members, there'd also been more than one attempted murder. And even though all of the traitors had been caught and dealt with, Wes still worried that someone had been overlooked and would try to attack the humans again.

Humans that meant the world to their mates, ones who'd also won the hearts of many of his clan members. The thought of them being forced to flee to another clan for safety was unfathomable.

His beast replied, *We have our trusted team watching over them and the clan. Not to mention the humans' mates will guard them, too. One night away won't hurt anyone.*

Wes mentally sighed. *You only say that because you're looking forward to people bidding on us.*

His inner dragon stood up a little taller inside his mind. *Damn straight. If we're lucky, it'll be a human female who'll help slake my itch.*

Your itch for sex is not *going to be fulfilled tonight.*

You never know. It could happen.

An approaching charity coordinator, a female ADDA employee he'd never met before in person but only through video chats, approached him and cut off his reply to his dragon.

The only good thing about the night so far was that one particular ADDA employee wasn't involved with the charity auction—a female named Ashley Swift.

Because if she were, Wes didn't know if he could go through with the auction. She was, after all, his true mate. Not that he could ever claim his fated mate since she worked with ADDA, and relationships were strictly forbidden between their employees and dragon-shifters.

And Wes's clan needed his leadership too much for him to throw it all away for a female, either. Some leaders might walk away for their true mate, but Wes had hundreds of people counting on him. That was more important than his own selfish desires.

His dragon, on the other hand, kept fighting tooth and nail for her.

Thank fuck Ashley wasn't here tonight. Because if she had been, his dragon would've fought against any other female winning them.

For once, it seemed as if Wes had a lucky break.

The ADDA female smiled up at him—her name was Jennifer Sakamoto if he remembered right—and he pushed all thoughts of Ashley aside.

She motioned toward the stage. "You're our final bid for the night and are up next. You have the cell phone we gave you and the special list of contact numbers, just in case anything goes wrong?"

Even though Wes was a clan leader, ADDA didn't

completely trust any dragon-shifter inside one of the human cities. Not even in a place like Reno, which was constantly full of tourists and its fair share of interesting people, meaning Wes's height and distinct tattoo would often go unnoticed.

His dragon snorted. *Until our pupils start flashing to slits.*

Ignoring his beast, Wes nodded. "I have both things, though I hope I don't need either of them."

"Good. Then just remember to smile and stay quiet on stage, and we'll do the rest." Jennifer paused and added, "Thank you again for doing this. The orphaned dragon program desperately needs all the money we can raise as more and more half-dragon babies are abandoned at our front doors."

The orphaned dragon program helped relocate babies left on ADDA's doorstep, usually by a human who'd had an unapproved fling with a dragon-shifter. "Of course. And remember what I said earlier—Pine-Rock is more than willing to foster some of them, too."

After bobbing her head, Jennifer turned, and he followed her to his final waiting spot at the side of the stage. Through the curtain, he heard the applause die down, and the emcee's voice filled the room again. "Thank you, Ms. Johnson, for your generous bid! Enjoy your night with the handsome young gentleman from Clan StoneRiver. Now, the next man up for a night on the town is a very special guest indeed. Have you ever wondered what a dragon-shifter clan leader is like? Well, ladies and gentlemen, the wait is over! Welcome our final participant, Wes Dalton, who is the leader of Clan PineRock."

Taking a deep breath, Wes entered the main stage and did his best to smile. The bright lights made it hard to see at first, but as everyone sat down and the clapping slowly ceased, his eyes adjusted, and he double blinked at the packed room.

He'd heard how the ADDA-sponsored orphan charity auctions were popular, but seeing it in person was different than hearing about it. There had to be somewhere between two and three hundred people in the room.

Most of which had some sort of numbered card in their hands. He wondered how many would bid for him.

His dragon shrugged his wings. *Most of them. We are the greatest catch of the evening.*

Just as the emcee began the bidding process, Wes noticed one of the females in the crowd lifting a numbered sign. The human was a familiar one with dark hair piled atop her head and dark blue eyes he'd never forget.

He stopped breathing. After all, he'd only ever seen Ashley Swift in her buttoned-down shirts and pants, but tonight she was in a tight-fitting black dress. A dress that revealed more creamy, pale skin than he'd ever seen from her before.

And she was staring right at him, her numbered card raised in the air.

She was bidding on him.

Both male and beast wanted to roar, rush off the stage, and make a beeline for her.

Ashley, their fated mate, should be the one who claimed their night. After so many years of saying he couldn't have her, a pounding need coursed through his body.

Both man and dragon wanted Ashley for one night, even if that was all he'd ever have.

The thought of her not winning made him clench his fingers into fists. She was so close and yet still so far.

As the bidding continued, he barely listened to the dollar amounts. He couldn't look away from Ashley's eyes, made all the brighter by her makeup.

Damn, she was beautiful. And while it was as dangerous as hell to wish it, he wished with everything he had for her to win.

However, he had no control over the situation, and he fucking hated it. Wes was used to being in charge, making decisions, and steering the future of his entire clan.

And now all he could do was wait and hope like hell that Ashley wanted to win this as much as he did.

Resisting a growl, Wes did his best to control his emotions and waited to see who won.

It was foolish for Ashley Swift to attend the special ADDA charity auction for many reasons. The place was full of dragon-shifters and other ADDA employees she was usually forbidden to dally with outside of work hours. Every other year, she'd been able to resist and stay home.

But not this time. No, this time there was someone in the auction she'd always wanted to know better. Ever since she'd met Wes Dalton over three years ago, she'd been dangerously drawn to him.

No, more than drawn. Whenever their eyes met, her heart raced, and it took a hell of a lot of effort just to keep breathing.

And that was just when discussing work issues and dry-as-bone protocols. She'd probably combust if they were ever alone together somewhere private.

True, there were drawbacks to being around him, too. He provoked her more than any person she knew, and he often stoked her temper. But he was also funny and cared deeply for his clan.

Just as she cared deeply for all her charges under the protection of ADDA.

Which meant neither of them could ever do more than trade barbs for a few minutes here and there. At least, until she'd finally figured out a loophole—the charity auction.

The rules and fine print allowed ADDA employees to bid since the charity was registered independently from their organization. Also, ADDA wanted to help raise as much money as possible to help the orphaned dragon children and didn't want to turn away potential donors.

So Ashley had decided to seize her only chance to be alone with him and bid on Wes Dalton. Since all she did was work or read, she'd saved up a lot of money over the last ten years at her job. And she'd gladly spend it to help a great cause and pretend she was just a normal human woman out on the town with a dragonman.

No rules, no restrictions, no job title. She could be just a woman for once.

A free woman who'd finally ended the farce of an engagement six months ago. She may not be able to ever have Wes, but she'd always want him. No other man could ever compare.

Tonight would have to be enough.

When Wes finally walked out on stage, all sexy in his button-up shirt and blazer, her jaw nearly dropped open.

She knew he was like most dragon-shifters and had a muscled body from so much flying. But damn, he looked good in more formal wear. Add in his auburn-colored hair, brown eyes, and chiseled jaw, and any straight woman would probably start drooling after him, too.

When Wes finally met her eyes, even from her spot in the middle of the room, she noticed how his pupils flashed. They did that a lot with her—the change signaling that his inner dragon was speaking to his human half—and not for the first time she wondered what his dragon talked about. Was it her? Or, about how much he wanted her to go away so that Wes could focus on his clan and finding his own true mate?

As a teenager, Ashley had hoped she was a dragon's

true mate. But the longer she worked inside ADDA, the more she grew wary of it becoming true in the present day. Because if she was one, she'd have to quit her job.

Then who the hell would she be? Work was her life, and no matter how much she loved books, reading wasn't exactly a career option.

However, as Wes continued to stare at her, never glancing away, she forgot about all that and shivered. Wes's eyes instantly flashed quicker.

Maybe he was focusing on her because she was familiar. Yes, that had to be it. Because in all their previous interactions, he'd never looked at her like this before—a mixture of heat and something she couldn't define.

To be honest, the lack of usual irritation in his gaze was a little unsettling.

The emcee's voice filled the room. After they finished introducing Wes, the bidding started.

Ashley raised her sign, but so did a number of other women. As the price went up, her competition went down.

And by the time the bid reached two thousand dollars, it was between her and one other woman.

Bring it, lady. Ashley had wanted the night with Wes before, but after his smoking-hot gaze and seeing his sexiness in that shirt and blazer, she would have him, no matter what it cost.

The bid reached five thousand and the other woman hesitated. After the last calls for more bids, the emcee slammed the small gavel and said, "We have a winner!

Number 203, come to the side of the stage to give your donation and collect your prize for the night."

After Ashley scooped up her purse and light jacket, she forced her gaze from Wes's and headed to the small table positioned to the left side of the stage. With each step she took, her heart raced faster.

Wes Dalton was hers. At least, for one night he was.

Thankfully due to the rules, there were plenty of boundaries to keep her from doing something stupid. Because without them and the threat of losing her job, she would throw her no one-night stand rule to the wind and try to seduce Wes.

No. Can't do it, Ash. Not worth it. To many of her colleagues, working for ADDA was a job to pay the bills and nothing more. However, to Ashley, it was a calling. She wanted a better future for humans and dragon-shifters. And there were so many changes left to usher in, ones that would require years to accomplish.

Sleeping with one dragon-shifter wasn't worth the untold amount of damage she'd do to others in the future if she were fired.

No, tonight would be about teasing Wes and having a good time. If nothing else, it could strengthen their working relationship. Yes, that's what she needed to focus on.

Ashley reached the table and went through the motions, writing her check, and getting her receipts. Once done, the woman helping her motioned toward a door off to the side. "When you're ready, he's waiting for you in there."

As soon as Ashley turned from the woman, she took a deep breath and stood a little taller. She hadn't cowed down to a dragon-shifter in a long time, and she wasn't going to let herself act any different around Wes tonight, either.

They'd have some fun, and Ashley could finally get the man out of her system before focusing back on her work.

That's right, just one night of fun, nothing else. And if Wes turned grumpy as he'd done in the past, she'd remind him that the bid was for a fun night out.

At that thought, she smiled. It seemed for once she really was the one in charge out of the pair of them. Wes would hate it, which made it all the more entertaining.

So Ashley headed toward the door and the dragonman waiting on the other side.

Chapter Two

Wes did his best not to fidget as he waited for Ashley to claim him, which was made more difficult by the fact his inner dragon was pacing inside their mind.

Wes growled, *Stop it. You're acting like this is going to be more than a one-night thing, and that's all it can be, dragon.*

But it's a night with our true mate. Maybe she won us for a reason, and there's a way to have her and still be leader of the clan.

You think I haven't thought of that, too?

However, despite searching through the dizzying fine print of the ADDA rules available to him—which wasn't all—and the laws surrounding all dragon-shifters in the US, he'd yet to find it. He wasn't a lawyer, though. And that gave him a sliver of hope that something existed to help. Maybe not for him, but for others.

His beast huffed. *Just don't actively try to make her mad or piss her off. I want this night to be different, to make an impact on her so that maybe she'll want to work with us to find a loophole. And so help me, if you fuck it up, I'll take control.*

You do that in a human city, and we'll be sent back to PineRock before we can say a word, forbidden to visit any human town or city for years.

It'll be worth it if I can get to better know our true mate.

As Wes tried to think of how to reply to that, the doorknob turned, and the door opened to reveal the tall, curvy form of Ashley Swift.

From across the room, she'd been beautiful. But as she walked closer to him, her hips swaying and her delicious scent of female mixed with vanilla reaching his nose, he stopped breathing.

Add in her pretty dark hair piled atop her head, and he wanted to growl, reach out, and pull her close.

His inner dragon laughed. *You want her just as much as I do.*

She stopped a few feet away from him, searching his gaze. He loved how she was nearly the same height as him. That may be tall for a human female—at about six feet—but perfect for him.

Tilting her head, she asked, "What's your dragon saying now?"

His dragon growled again. *Tell her I want to strip off her clothes and lick every luscious inch of her body.*

Wes barely resisted clearing this throat. "That you look nice tonight."

She snorted. "Nice? And here I was going to say you look sexy, but I guess I can revise it to nice as well."

Her regular demeanor broke the spell, making the rational sections of his brain and tongue disconnect from one another as he said, "I figured saying you look good enough to eat would be a bad idea, even if I know you like honesty."

She clutched her purse tighter against her side, her eyes searching his.

Fuck, he'd probably said the wrong thing. But it was hard to be anything but himself around this female

It was going to be a hell of a long night.

"Honest is better than 'nice,' for sure." She motioned toward the exit off to the side. "Let's get our night started, shall we? I was thinking a bar and maybe something supernormal, like darts or pool."

It was on the tip of his tongue to bark he couldn't have more than one drink at any bar by law but held back. Ashley had paid a small fortune for his company, and the money was for a good cause.

He'd be nice to her if it killed him.

Wes waved her on. "After you."

She raised an eyebrow. "I'm not sure how to handle you being nice to me. Keep it up, and I'll have to work extra hard to provoke you until I bring out the man I want to spend the evening with."

Ashley *wanted* him to argue and trade barbs?

As she walked ahead of him, he quickly pushed that thought aside and took the opportunity to study her ass and hips while no one else was around.

His dragon blasted a thought about taking her from

behind, but Wes ignored it. He had to keep some boundaries.

So he fell back on words. "So now you'd rather I be a bastard and start an argument?"

She glanced over her shoulder, and a tendril of hair came loose from her updo, lightly caressing the bare skin of her shoulder. Damn, he wondered which was softer—her hair or her skin.

Raising her brows, Ashley replied, "I've called you a bastard before, but in reality, you aren't one, Wes. Just be yourself and don't dare walk on eggshells around me now, of all times."

He grunted, unsure of how to take the compliment. "You're a strong female who can handle her own. I won't fucking treat you like a porcelain doll."

She smiled, but quickly turned away from him to reach for the theater exit door. The sudden loss of her gaze made him want to reach out, turn her around, and lose himself in her eyes again.

He resisted a sigh. Yes, it was going to be a really long fucking night.

Once Ashley opened the door, sounds from the main casino floor filled the air—old-fashioned slot machines clicking, various game-like spinning sounds, and even a few winner bells.

Add in the chatter and music blasting from some corner in the building, and he wanted to cover his ears against the racket.

The bombardment reminded Wes why he stayed

away from Reno. Dragon-shifters had supersensitive senses, and there was too much fucking noise.

Ashley stopped just outside the door and faced him. Despite all the human, food, and various other smells he didn't want to think about, hers surrounded him, her female musk making his cock hard.

Thank fuck his blazer covered it up.

She spoke quietly, knowing he'd hear it despite the noise. "How about we forget clan and ADDA politics for the night? Pretend we're on a first date."

Even though his dragon screamed yes, Wes asked, "Is that wise?"

She rolled her eyes. "Then what should it be? Act as if we're two guys out on the town? That may be a little hard as I refuse to be a wingman for you to pick up some human chick to bang."

He swore there was jealousy threaded into her voice, but he didn't dare hope. "Being clan leader takes up all of my free time. As soon as my evening with you is up, I'll be heading straight back to PineRock. I have no desire to go looking for a female. They're huge wastes of time."

Wes nearly winced. In his past experiences, when females only wanted a night with him because he was clan leader, they had been disappointments, yes. But he shouldn't have said that to Ashley. He actually looked forward to spending time with her.

"Well, isn't that nice," she drawled. "Females are a waste of time. You aren't very good with words when you talk about anything but clan politics, are you?"

His beast piped up. *You're screwing this up.*

You think I don't know that? Even though it shouldn't matter.

Ashley placed a hand on his arm, and despite the shirt and blazer, her touch seared his skin.

And for a few seconds, they stared at each other again, everything else fading away until all he heard was her breaths and her heart beating.

What he wouldn't give to kiss her, just once, and see if she lived up to his fantasies.

But since kissing her on the lips would set off a mate-claim frenzy—a nonstop sex marathon that lasted until she was pregnant—not even a playful kiss could be on the table.

Wes finally took a step back, dislodging her grip on his arm. The action snapped him back to the present. "Just tell me where you want to go, and I'll try to be fun."

Ashley rolled her eyes. "Fine, Mr. Stick-to-a-Plan. There's a bar nearby, one that allows dragon-shifters."

Perhaps, but then it'd only give him one drink before kicking him out.

Such were the stupid rules dragon-shifters had to live by in the US.

He gestured ahead and made an effort not to be a dick again. "Then lead on, my lady."

She grabbed his hand. "Since I know where we're going, follow me. And don't let go. I don't need any of the losing bidders from the auction rushing up and attempting to steal you away."

Her skin against his made both man and beast hum.

It was dangerous to hold her hand, but right then and there, someone would have to cut off his arm before he released her. "I won't let go. Should I pinkie promise or are my words enough?"

Snorting, she murmured, "Pinkie promises aren't very leader-like," before she guided them out of the casino and down the street. All the while Wes wondered if she was anywhere near as affected by them holding hands as he was.

His cockstand wasn't going anywhere for the foreseeable future.

Behaving for even a few hours around the female was going to be harder than any clan leadership trial.

ASHLEY TRIED to be casual about holding Wes's hand, but sparks raced down her arms and ended between her legs.

It was embarrassing enough that he could probably smell her arousal—damn dragons and their super noses —but it also made her realize how attracted she was to him.

Dangerously so.

And now she'd proposed bringing alcohol into the mix? Ashley was going to have to be careful or she might end up doing something extremely stupid.

She spotted the bar she wanted, *Deuces Wild*, and reluctantly released his hand to head inside.

The second she stepped into the warm room filled

with music and conversation, quite a few heads turned toward her. However, their gazes quickly moved over to Wes, many of them turning suspicious.

Glancing to Wes, she noticed he'd already put on the mandatory pin of a dragon with outstretched wings on the front of his jacket, the one he had to wear inside human establishments and meetings that weren't run by ADDA.

She hated the dragon outline in bright orange against the dark color of his blazer and wished she could toss it into the trash.

But hiding a dragon-shifter's true identity was against the law, and she didn't want to have Wes carted off to jail. Because even if he could manage to keep his eyes from flashing to hide his identity, the owner of the bar had a part-time dragon-shifter security guard, one who sat incognito in the corner, who would be able to tell.

She gestured with her head toward the bar. The reason she'd picked this place was because she knew the owner and most of the bartenders. After all, she'd been the one to convince Natasha to open her doors to dragon patrons and even get her part-time dragon security guard position approved.

And as luck had it, Natasha was behind the bar tonight. The woman with brown skin and black hair streaked with blue smiled at her before saying, "Given the fuck-me heels and dress, I don't think you're here on business tonight, are you, Ash?"

Natasha's eyes darted back to Wes again as Ashley

resisted smoothing her skirt. If Wes had noticed the revealing black dress, he hadn't said a word. She replied, "No business tonight, but it's not what you think, either, Tasha." She gestured toward Wes. "I won him in the dragon orphan auction and came here for a few hours of fun."

Natasha studied Wes and smiled slowly. The action made Ashley grip her purse tighter to keep her arms in place. Otherwise, she might try to thread an arm through the dragonman's to signal Wes was off-limits.

Even though that wasn't technically true.

The bar owner said, "Welcome, dragonman. As long as you don't break the rules, we'll get along great. What'll you guys have?"

Wes looked over at Ashley. "What are you drinking?"

If Ashley were playing it safe, she'd go for a light beer. But screw that, tonight was special. So she said, "Long Island iced tea, extra strong."

Natasha snorted. "Careful, as my extra strong can make even linebackers wobble on their feet."

Ashley shrugged. "For the next few days, I'm on vacation. So what the hell?" She glanced back at Wes. "You?"

"Whiskey, neat."

Yes, she could see him drinking whiskey when he was alone, sipping to help take the edge off his stressful job.

"You got it," Natasha stated and turned away to make the drinks.

Ashley's gaze fell to Wes's lips. She wondered what the combination of man and whiskey would taste like.

Wes cleared his throat. "Careful, Ashley. You're all but begging me to break every rule there is and kiss you."

She met his gaze again. But instead of amusement, his pupils flashed between round and slitted, heat filling his eyes.

Damn, had all of Wes's bickering and challenging over the years hidden something else?

Natasha put the drinks down, and Ashley shook her head to clear it of such thoughts. She plucked out some money and paid for the drinks.

Wes growled, "I can pay for myself."

"Not tonight." She leaned in, picking up her drink and whispering to his ears only. "Tonight, you're my date, so I'm footing the bill."

"I have no say in this, do I?"

She smiled. "None. You know how stubborn I can be."

"Better than anyone," he murmured.

She laughed and motioned toward his drink. "Well, you're about to see another side to me, too—the competitive part. We're going to play either pool or darts. Your pick."

Swiping his whiskey from the bar, he asked, "Which are you better at?"

"Darts."

"Then darts it is." He leaned closer, his scent invading her nose. "Because it'll be that much sweeter when I win."

The words brought up another image, one of him winning control when she was naked and under him.

And Ashley pressed her legs closer together, hoping he couldn't tell how damn sexy that was to her.

But then his pupils flashed faster and she knew he'd scented her.

Taking a sip of her drink, she leaned away from him and walked toward the section with the dartboards against the back wall.

On impulse, she added an extra swing to her hips and could feel Wes's gaze on her ass.

The responsible thing would be to win at darts, down her drink, and end the night early.

However, as she took another sip of her uber strong drink, she decided that wasn't going to happen. She wanted to make the most of her one and only night with Wes Dalton.

If she could get them somewhere private, then there were a few things they could do without fully breaking the rules set forth in ADDA's guidebook.

But she needed to get Wes relaxed enough to agree. One drink would do nothing to him, with his fast dragon metabolism. Which meant she'd have to try and do it some other way.

And so her latest challenge began.

Chapter Three

W es watched Ashley's body sway as she walked away, his dragon growling and pacing inside his head at the sight. His beast said, *She's inviting us to claim her. Can't you see it?*

Just because she's attracted to us doesn't mean she's going to throw away everything she knows to sleep with us.

Then take her away from this bar. If we fly to one of our secret spots, no one will know what happens. And true, we can't kiss her mouth, but there are plenty of other things we could do. Like lick that sweet honey between her thighs.

He resisted groaning. *Don't tempt me, dragon.*

At least think about it. Punishments only happen to those who get caught.

And damn his beast, they both knew there were dragons and humans alike who found ways to sneak off and never be found out.

Not that a clan leader should ever chance it.

Ignoring his beast, he picked up his pace. On the way toward the dart-playing area, he finally spotted the dragon-shifter he'd scented. The male was unfamiliar to him. But even if he hadn't been wearing his designated dragon pin on his shirt—which he was—the tall, muscled build and flashing eyes gave him away.

Wes nodded, and the male returned the gesture before turning his gaze back toward the bar area.

Filing away the man's description for later—Wes wanted to know who worked here since some of his clan members came to this bar—he closed the small distance to where Ashley stood next to a round, high table not far from the dart-playing area. While he noticed the humans scurrying away from the section, he ignored them. Only the female across from him mattered. "So who goes first, and from what point count are we playing?"

Ashley raised an eyebrow. "I didn't expect you to play darts, let alone know the rules."

"Why? Because I'm clan leader?" He leaned over, resting an elbow on the table, and moved his head closer to Ashley's. "Here's a secret—I wasn't always clan leader. And like most males, once I hit twenty-one, I couldn't wait to visit my first human bar."

She leaned a fraction closer, and it took every bit of strength he had not to stare at her cleavage. "And how did that go?"

He smiled. "Not as awesome as I thought it would. I had my ass handed to me at pool, I downed the remainder of my drink in frustration, and they promptly tossed my butt onto the sidewalk."

Ashley laughed, the sound making the female even more irresistible to both man and beast. "It's hard to imagine anyone tossing you into the street."

"Let's just say it never happened again. Although sometimes I swear you try to do an equivalent level of ass-handing with useless ADDA paperwork."

She tsked, and his gaze zeroed in on her full lips. He couldn't tear his eyes away as she said, "No work stuff, remember?"

He stared some more, and Ashely bit her bottom lip. Damn, he'd fantasized about doing the same with his own teeth.

His dragon spoke up. *If you were strong enough to talk with her and tell her she's our true mate, it could be a reality.*

No, it can't.

As if burned, Wes moved back to standing and faced the dart-playing area. "Point count?"

Ashley sighed. "Sometimes your topic changes give me whiplash."

Since he couldn't exactly say "Hey, I want to kiss you and then fuck you senseless, over and over again, a tag team between my dragon and me, until you're pregnant and carry my scent. Are you cool with that?" Wes instead cleared his throat. "I'm excited to beat you, is all. You tend to have the upper hand with ADDA regulations, but I can win this."

"Oh, ho, so the dick swinging has started." He

couldn't help but glance at Ashley and saw her roll her shoulders back. "Bring it, dragonman. Because I can win that contest, too."

Wes couldn't help but smile. "Then hurry up with the rules, missy, so we can settle this."

"Missy, huh? All right, boyo, let's play from 301 the first time as a warm-up. I'll even let you go first."

Normally, he'd insist on Ashley throwing first. But if she was going to throw down about her abilities, then he'd test her truly, no holds barred. Picking up his darts from the cup on the table, he moved to the standing area on the floor and lined up his first shot.

Even though he could throw it straight away, he lingered a few extra seconds, more than aware of Ashley's gaze on his back.

As blood rushed south, Wes decided to win as quickly as possible so he could get her somewhere private. No, he couldn't kiss her or risk thrusting his cock inside her, but there were other things he could try with the female to ease his curiosity.

Because tonight was all he'd ever have with his true mate. And for a few hours, Wes was going to be just a male and not a clan leader.

Ignoring his dragon's roar of approval, he tossed the dart and grinned as it hit dead center. He looked over his shoulder and said with a grin, "Now I'm at 251."

Ashley glared and he laughed.

If not for the reward of being alone with the female, he'd tease her endlessly and do a little trash talking.

However, he wanted his true mate alone. So Wes lined up his next shot and hit the bull's-eye again.

ASHLEY KNEW she should be mentally preparing for her throws, but there was no way she could ignore the six-foot-plus frame of muscled dragon sexiness in front of her. As Wes threw his first dart, his muscles bulged under his clothes. While she'd never seen him without a shirt, her imagination didn't have trouble sketching it out.

Damn, she wanted a night with Wes. And for more than darts and drinks.

Stop it, Ash. One night of foolishness can ruin your career.

While the reminder helped to cool down her hormones a fraction, the alcohol running through her veins countered most of it.

Asking for a strong drink had been her first mistake. And if things kept going as they had, it wouldn't be her last.

After his first bull's-eye, she barely paid attention to the throws and watched how he flicked the dart with little effort. Wes eventually turned toward her, a triumphant gleam in his eye. It was only then she looked around him to the dartboard and groaned. "Three bull's-eyes in a row? How is that even possible?"

"With my superior eyesight and reflexes, you don't stand a chance, human."

Standing up tall, Ashley shimmied her skirt down and

did her best to ignore Wes's flashing pupils. Good, let him notice her. Maybe if she worked it enough, he'd lose his concentration and have some shitty throws.

She answered, "The night is young."

Walking by him, her arm brushed his, and she nearly sucked in a breath. Thank goodness dragon-shifters couldn't read minds because then he'd know that if he took off his shirt, she'd not be able to concentrate worth a damn.

Her darts in hand, she lined up her throw. No, she didn't have superhero-like senses, but she'd learned to be awesome at darts to win against some of the good ol' boys inside the American Department of Dragon Affairs.

When the dart landed in the center, she nearly jumped for joy but decided her heels weren't stable enough for it. One of the trade-offs for sexiness, for sure.

Just as she lifted her next dart, a light caress danced down her other arm. Electricity sizzled from her skin and ended between her thighs.

Ashely dropped the dart and it clattered to the floor.

A male chuckle filled her ear. "You didn't say we couldn't play dirty."

Wes. Turning her head to meet his gaze, her heart skipped a beat. The lazy smile and humor in his eyes transformed his usually handsome face into movie star territory. "Who are you and what have you done with Wes Dalton?"

He leaned closer, his hot breath dancing against her cheek as he replied, "Wes the male is very much here.

The clan leader part is taking a very, very short vacation. Maybe only for an hour or two." He ran his finger down her arm again, and this time she shivered at his warm, slightly rough touch. "Maybe we should take advantage of it."

She blinked and then laughed. "Are you trying to be sexy or something? Because it's so not you."

He frowned. "What the hell are you talking about?"

She lowered her voice to mimic him. "Maybe we should take advantage of it. Come on, baby, let's have a good time." He opened his mouth to protest, but Ashley beat him to it, her voice once again her own. "Let me ask you something—do you want to know the reason I bid for you and was determined to win you?"

His frown eased. "Why did you?"

She whispered for his ears only. "Because if you were a regular man and I was a regular woman, I know for a fact we would've slept together already. Maybe even dated. But since all of that is forbidden—not to mention we both have too much to lose—this was the best I could do. One night of fun before we go back to trading barbs about policy and reports." She dared to place a hand on his chest. "So just be you tonight, Wes. There's no need to impress me or try to be some guy you think I want, okay?"

Well, the alcohol had done its work, it seemed. The truth was out there.

And so Ashley searched Wes's gaze and waited to see how he'd reply.

WES SOMEHOW MANAGED to block out his dragon's demands once Ashley stated her truth—if she could've had him, she would have.

Why did she have to go and say that? It would make staying away from her and not kissing her that much harder. She wanted him, and he sure as hell wanted her.

His dragon flashed an image of them tangled in bed, Wes thrusting hard as he claimed Ashley's mouth at the same time.

His already hard cock turned to stone.

But for once, he didn't tell his dragon to stop.

Afraid Ashley would move away once the enormity of the words hit her, he placed his hand over hers and decided what the hell, he'd be honest, too. "I have a truth, too, if you want to hear it. But fair warning—it'll change everything."

She tilted her head, a few wisps of dark hair escaping over her shoulder. It took everything Wes had not to lean over and blow the strands away before placing his lips on her bared skin.

Her husky voice rolled over him as she said, "Tell me, Wes. That way I don't feel like such an idiot for blurting out how I imagined us naked together."

Okay, she hadn't said that exactly. More images flashed into his mind—Wes taking her from behind, against a wall, in the shower.

And she wouldn't be docile and only out to please

him, either, simply because he was clan leader. No, his human would be as fierce as him and not hold back. Part of him wanted her to scratch his skin and leave a mark, just to remind him she'd been in his bed.

And just like that, all the years of trying to ignore how much he wanted her faded away.

His dragon growled. *Tell her and then convince her she is ours to protect, to hold, to fuck, and so much more.*

A tiny bit of rationality returned to his brain. *We can't go that far.*

Why not? I bet she has a way around it.

Maybe, but let's take this one step at a time.

Before Wes could lose his nerve, he leaned closer and murmured, "You're my true mate, Ashley Swift. If there was any way to have you that didn't result in us both giving up what we treasure most, we'd be home and a lot less dressed right now."

Her breath hitched as her nails lightly dug into his shirt.

What he wouldn't give to have those nails scoring his back.

Fuck, his control was slipping.

Ashley replied before he could even begin to put it back into place. "I didn't think dragons could resist their true mates."

"Many can't, but I'm not most males, Ashley." He moved to her ear. "Although you saying that you want to fuck me and maybe even date me cracked my control a little. So tell me—what happens next? Is there a way for us to be together that I don't know about? Do you never want to see me again and then transfer to somewhere like Florida? Tell me what you want so that I can start making plans."

His dragon hummed in approval, but all Wes could think about was how he'd screwed up. ADDA employees and dragon-shifters simply didn't mix. The rules were set up that way specifically.

However, he'd said the words, and he sure as hell wasn't taking them back.

Whatever Ashley said in the next minute or so would determine his future.

Chapter Four

Ashley's heart thundered to the point she was sure any dragon-shifter within a mile radius could hear it.

Sure, she'd figured Wes was attracted to her, especially after his heated glances tonight. But she'd never imagined she was his true mate.

According to every ADDA report she'd read, dragon-shifters had a hard time staying away from their fated male or female. And even the strong ones avoided touching their true mate lest they trigger their dragon's need for sex. She sure as hell hadn't heard of any of them holding a true mate close and keeping their control solidly in place.

And yet, Wes had his hand over hers, his mouth at her ear, and hadn't slipped into any mate-claim frenzy or frantic need to fuck her until she was pregnant.

She'd known he was strong, but he had turned out to be far stronger than she'd imagined.

What she wouldn't give to say, "Yes! Take me home right now and claim me."

However, doing so would signal the end of her job with the four dragon clans in the greater Tahoe area. Maybe to some that wouldn't be a big deal, but Ashley had been ushering in all kinds of changes over the last couple of years.

Could she really give it up and all but let the dragons fend for themselves?

Something niggled at the back of her mind. Something about special allowances for clan leaders in good standing. However, before she could think harder on it, let alone reply to Wes, a pair of unfamiliar male voices filled the air. "Step away from the woman, fucking dragon trash. The poor lady is going to need a shower now, five times over, just to get rid of your stench."

Wes leaned back slowly, but before he could reply, Ashley stood tall and placed a hand on his arm to stay him.

The appearances of the two men in their thirties or forties were unremarkable—average height, slightly overweight, with jeans and T-shirts. However, it was the identical tattoos they each had on the backs of their hands that caught her attention. The symbol was seared into her memory from the earliest days of her ADDA training: an eagle clutching a rifle in one claw and an American flag in the other.

Shit. They were part of the "America for Humans Only League," which were the biggest pains in ADDA's asses. Their acronym was fitting—AHOL. Although she thought asshole was too tame a word for them. Regardless, most people just called them the League.

Their primary goal was to banish all dragon-shifters in the USA to either Canada or Mexico, and often formed their own groups to try and make that a reality.

If she wasn't careful, things could get out of hand. Fast.

Keeping her voice even, she stated, "This woman has a mind of her own, thank you very much. And it's you two who should leave."

The slightly taller man with unshaven cheeks raised his brows. "He's brainwashed you, baby. Good thing we're here to help you. Come with us, and we'll remind you why dragons are the enemy. They only want us around to give them money, children, and land. They're not to be trusted."

Ashley hoped those lines didn't work on women or men in the company of dragons. Because if so, ADDA's job of making the League a designated hate group would be that much harder. The press would have a field day with even a handful of humans saying how they'd been saved from the dragons because of the League's intervention and guidance.

Wes grunted. "The lady said you should leave. I'd listen to her."

The other man, the one with gray in his hair, took a

step toward Wes. "Don't talk to me, you fucking monster. You shouldn't be allowed in the same room as any human, let alone touch one."

Just as Ashley expected, Wes's pupils flashed. His dragon was most likely pissed.

Wes shrugged. "I haven't broken any rules, so I'm staying."

The pair of League members took a step closer, but then another man moved to stand between them and Ashley and Wes—Natasha's part-time dragon employee, Brad Harper. His gruff voice stated to the human men, "It's time for you two to leave for the night."

Their eyes darted to the dragon pin affixed to the tall, muscled dragonman's shirt and back to his face. The unshaven one crossed his arms over his chest and said, "Not until this piece of scum is separated from this lady."

As both of the dragonmen growled simultaneously, Ashley tried to think of what to do. She couldn't let either dragon-shifter be banned simply for trying to help her.

She moved in front of the dragonmen and put her arms out wide to her sides. It seemed her wish of a night spent being a woman and not working for ADDA had ended. "I'm a high-ranking ADDA employee. So unless you want me to call the police and personally file claims of harassment against these dragonmen, you'll do as Brad says and leave."

The two human guys narrowed their eyes. However, before either one could say a word, another man appeared at their side. Despite his casual jeans and button-down shirt, the quality of his clothes and his expensive watch told her he had money. And after a second, she realized who he was—Duncan Parrish. A powerful business owner in his own right, he also had the ear of not only a member of the Nevada Gaming Control Board but one of Nevada's senators as well.

In other words, he had connections that might surpass her own.

Duncan cleared his throat. "Excuse my brother-in-law and his friend. We've had a lot to drink and should be going, Miss…?"

She didn't want to give her name but knew she had to since she'd stated her ADDA connection. "Ashley Swift."

"Right, Miss Swift." Duncan lowered his voice. "I'd suggest you and your friend leave right after us, though. The room is turning against you."

From the corner of her eyes, she could see people starting to gather. After all the trouble and backlash Natasha had faced upon opening her doors to dragon-shifters, Ashley owed it to the woman to avoid any more scandal. She lowered her arms. "Once I see you guys leave, we'll wait a few minutes and follow suit."

Duncan bobbed his head. "You have my word that we won't follow you."

She didn't know shit about the value of his word but kept her well-rehearsed smile in place. "Sounds like a plan."

As they left, Duncan whispered something to the

unshaven man, who then looked over his shoulder with a sinister grin.

Shit. If Duncan Parrish was somehow involved with the League, then it could spell trouble for her, for the dragon-shifters, and for anyone who worked with ADDA in the greater Reno area. Hell, maybe even in all of Nevada.

The only good thing was that Wes's clan was located in California, which gave him some protection from Parrish.

Wes whispered into her ear, "I'd say thank you, but I don't want your ego to get too big tonight."

At his light teasing, she turned away from the trio of men leaving and smiled up at Wes. "I deal with worse on a daily basis." She looked at the bar's security guard. "Thanks, Brad. We'll be okay from here."

Brad nodded and left to conduct one of his checks around the room. When they were alone, Wes murmured, "We need to talk in private. Where can we go?"

It had to be eating at Wes to not know everything and be in control like he was back on PineRock. But this was Ashley's territory, and she wouldn't feel bad about that. She glanced at Natasha, and the woman met her gaze. Ashley nodded toward the back, the bar owner bobbed her head to give permission, and Ashley took Wes's hand. "This way."

As she led him out the back door and down an alley to another side street, she did her best to focus on what had just happened with the two League members and Duncan Parrish. Because if she let herself remember the conversation right before that, she'd lose focus. And considering how powerful Duncan's reach was in Reno, she couldn't afford to be distracted until Wes was safely back on PineRock.

WES'S DRAGON paced inside his head, snarling every few seconds as Ashley led them to some unknown destination.

His beast spoke up. *We should've been able to challenge those humans to defend our mate's honor.*

And be thrown in prison as a result? You know any type of altercation in the human sphere doesn't end well for a dragon-shifter, even if the human was the one to start it.

That's why Ashley needs to live on PineRock. It's the only way we can protect her.

His instinctive side agreed. The looks and words from that smarmy asshat who'd tried to act the hero back in the bar rang warning bells inside Wes's head. Wes was pretty sure they'd see him again at some point. And when that happened, the fucker would no doubt be the furthest thing from a hero.

Even if he lacked the League tattoo, Wes suspected the human male was aligned with them in some way.

Ashley finally stopped at a small, red car. She gestured toward the passenger side. "Get in."

The car was different from the one she used for ADDA—it had to be her personal one—and sliding into the seat, he smiled at the unicorn plushie sitting on the dashboard. The butterfly crystal hanging from the rearview mirror glinted slightly pink in the pale light. He snorted. "Where are the rainbows and kittens?"

She gestured toward the back. "Right there."

Sure enough, there was a kitten stuffed animal on the back seat and some butterfly and rainbow heart stickers on the rear window. It was such a contrast to her usually dark, nondescript shirt and trouser outfits she wore for work. "I'm almost afraid to see what your home looks like."

She winked. "Well, it's your lucky day because you're about to find out."

His dragon hummed. *Good. We'll have her alone and can convince her she needs to be our mate.*

Ignoring his beast, he replied, "It'd be safer for both of us back on PineRock."

She pushed the Start button, and the car roared to life. "My place is closer. And there's no way I'd be able to concentrate all the way to PineRock in the dark. Even if I've been there a thousand times, the roads are little more than dirt sometimes."

"That's by design, as you well know. To keep the League and other unwanted visitors away."

She pulled into the road and, without moving her gaze from it, said, "Regardless, I should be just under the legal limit right now since I didn't finish even half my drink, and I don't want to test my reflexes if I can help it."

"You should let me drive. It'd take half a bottle to get me drunk, and I barely had a few sips."

To his surprise, she pulled over and faced him. "Will it be a battle for you to follow my directions? I don't want to waste time with male bullshit about finding things on your own."

He smiled. Wes would never tire of her directness. "You're one of the few females I'd take orders from."

He hadn't meant for the words to be chock-full of innuendo, but they ended up that way. And as they stared at each other, he heard Ashley's heart rate skyrocket.

His dragon spoke up. *Hurry up and change places. I want her alone.*

Even though Wes would never allow his dragon to get out of control, he agreed they should hurry. To make sure Ashley was safe and nothing more, or so he tried to reassure himself.

Quickly exiting the car, he was at the driver's side before Ashley had done more than unfasten her seat belt. He opened the door. "Are you going to scoot over or climb out? Either way, make a decision because you can't sit in my lap."

She snorted. "You'd like that, wouldn't you? But it'd defeat the purpose of not getting into an accident. You'd have no blood left in your brain to make any decisions at all."

What he wouldn't give to stand there trading barbs

until he could haul her against him and kiss the living shit out of her.

As she climbed over to the passenger seat, her dress sneaking up precariously high, Wes's heart skipped a beat, and his cock turned hard again.

He needed to get his female safe and do everything he could to make her his. There had to be a way where Wes could protect her, and she could still help his kind.

Ashley gestured toward the now-empty seat, and Wes sat down. After they were both buckled in and he'd shifted the car into Drive, he asked, "Where to?"

As she rattled off directions, he did his best to focus only on the road. Because the small glimpse he'd risked a few seconds ago showed her dress still riding high and her lovely, pale thighs on display.

Yep, Wes was truly a bastard right now. He should be thinking of her safety, and yet all he could think about were those thighs wrapped around his head while he made her scream with his tongue.

His dragon chimed in. *We might yet have that tonight.*

I doubt it, dragon. Once we iron out a few details with Ashley, we're heading home.

His beast pouted but remained silent. That told Wes volumes—his dragon would be hatching a plan of his own, which meant Wes would have to resist both Ashley and his dragon so he could do his duty as clan leader.

His night wasn't going to end as he'd hoped. But it also was long from over.

Chapter Five

A shley did her best to sober up on the ride home. She'd been honest about not being drunk—she may not be twenty-one any longer, but she still had a decent tolerance—but it was easier to think if she didn't have to concentrate on the road.

Not to mention she could sneak glimpses of Wes's profile from the corner of her eye as a passenger. No matter if it was in shadow or highlighted by a streetlamp, the strong jaw, nose, and his full lips were sexy as hell.

Which made being in a short dress, inside a car with a dragonman with supersensitive senses a real test of controlling her lady parts.

But as she let her thoughts drift to Duncan, the League, and even for a few seconds to what Wes had revealed to her about being his true mate, her focus shifted from her libido to her new set of problems.

Ashley lived in Reno, Nevada because of ADDA's

main base in the region there. Once Wes returned to PineRock, and provided his clan members didn't cross the California-Nevada border any time soon, they should be relatively safe from Duncan's political reach in Nevada. However, Ashley would constantly be looking over her shoulder. She had no idea if the League had made her their latest target or not, but living in a big city where she didn't know whom to trust wasn't exactly ideal.

She'd already taken extra precautions over the years when going out since working for ADDA could be challenging at times, even with just regular humans. But the possible danger had become a lot more personal all of a sudden with the encounter in the bar.

Her own safety wasn't the only issue, either. If she didn't get this mess cleared up ASAP, it could hurt both the dragon-shifters and all the human owners who'd risked so much to open their establishments to all patrons, too. Because if the League targeted Ashley, they'd follow her. Which meant her regular visits would put others in danger.

The question was, how could she ensure anyone's safety going forward?

Rubbing her forehead, Ashley realized this would be the biggest headache of her career in years.

Wes's voice cut through her thoughts. "I'm guessing this wasn't what you had planned when you won me for a night out, is it?"

She shook her head. "No. But I'll figure it all out somehow. I always do."

Wes paused a moment before replying, "You don't have to do it alone, Ashley. I'm here. I'll always be here."

Given her colleagues and web of contacts, she didn't have to go it alone, but she usually did. It was easier that way. No one could betray you or break a promise with disastrous consequences.

However, as she stared at Wes's profile with the light playing on his face, she could imagine a life where Wes was at her side, giving support and suggestions until they were both old and gray. Yes, he was hot, but there was so much more to Wes Dalton that attracted her.

The niggle from before, about clan leaders in good standing, reared its head again. Although why it surfaced now, when she had a shit-ton of other problems to deal with on her plate, she had no idea.

A small voice in her mind whispered, *Because you want him.*

Hell, she'd ended her engagement with her ex because of her feelings about Wes. But admitting that to the dragonman out loud wasn't a step she was quite ready for.

She finally replied, "Thanks, but I'm not even sure of what kind of help I need right now, so I can't exactly ask for it."

The corner of his lips ticked up. "Honest even now."

She blew out a breath. "Which you seem to like, but it won't work with a guy like Duncan Parrish."

"So that's his name. Tell me more about him."

As she explained his payday loan empire in Reno and

recent expansion to Vegas, as well as his higher political connections, she added, "But I had no idea his brother-in-law was a member of the League. That's going to spell trouble, I can feel it."

Wes moved a hand from the wheel and tentatively held it above Ashley's thigh. However, he quickly pulled it away as if burned and gripped the steering wheel tighter. "Which is why you need to stay somewhere safe until you think of a plan." She opened her mouth, but he beat her to it, threading his voice with the dominance clan leaders liked to use on a regular basis. "I know you're a strong, capable female, Ash. That's not the issue. But the League doesn't always follow the law, as you well know. The only safe place for you right now is with a dragon clan."

She almost nodded. It was true—the League talked big but rarely went after a group, let alone an entire clan of dragons. They preferred picking their targets off alone or in couples, drugging them unconscious, and smuggling them across borders.

It seemed ridiculous on the surface since a dragon could just fly back. However, things got a hell of a lot trickier once a dragon-shifter crossed international borders without permission. In recent years, the US Government hadn't allowed them back in at all due to the anti-dragon faction having a majority in Congress.

Which made her think the League had grown more powerful in recent years and had influence beyond what ADDA could've imagined possible.

Still, running wasn't exactly her style. "I think what

you're saying is that you want me to stay with you, but I can't."

Wes raised his brows. "Why not?"

The way he stated it, so matter-of-factly, made her blink. "You can't be serious, Wes. I'm not a researcher and don't do long-term observations. If I stay on your clan—especially if word got out that I'm your true mate —I won't merely be demoted, I'll be fired."

"So you'd rather keep your job but lose your life?"

She narrowed her eyes. "It's not that simple."

Wes glanced at her, his pupils flashing. "For once I agree with my dragon—humans can be illogical sometimes."

Ashley leaned forward a little. "Look, maybe some women go all gaga for your alpha attitude and desire to protect. But I've been on my own a long time, Wes. And I've worked my ass off to get where I am. Just walking away would be like losing half of who I am. Not to mention it would hurt all the dragon clans near Tahoe for the foreseeable future since most ADDA employees don't care about your kind as much as I do. How would that sit on your conscience?"

If she thought to knock him back with that, she was mistaken. Wes grunted. "How about staying for a few days then? Tori just had her baby anyway, and checking in on her is one of your duties. It's not unusual for an ADDA employee to stay a short while to watch a new human parent on a dragon's lands. Maybe if you're lucky,

Gaby will have her kid a little early, and then you could stay even longer."

She opened her mouth but quickly closed it. He was right—it was pretty much par for the course to observe new human parents of baby dragon-shifters. True, she'd briefly checked on the human woman named Victoria Santos recently, but Ashley hadn't filed the report yet. Also, Gaby was a dragon-shifter mated to a human and was due soon. Both fell under her jurisdiction.

Could a few days really buy her enough time to think of a better plan?

Probably. Especially if she could bounce ideas off Wes and his clan's chief of security, Cristina Juarez.

She crossed her arms over her chest. "I could manage to stay for a few days, but only with some ground rules."

A smile danced on his lips. "Of course you'd have rules. Let's hear them."

She raised a finger. "First and foremost, I won't be staying with you specifically."

He raised his brows. "Did I ever say you would be?"

"No, but given how you revealed I'm your true mate tonight, it had to have crossed your mind."

His voice was even as he replied, "What I want and what I do are two very different things."

The last traces of any alcohol-related haziness cleared her brain as she realized something that had been in front of her all along. Wes also gave up a lot to keep his position and fight for his clan.

Just how hard was it for him to resist her this long? They'd known each other for years.

She already respected him for his work, but that respect ticked up a few notches.

Softening her voice, she said, "I'm sorry. I don't intentionally try to be such a pain in the ass. My guard and defensiveness just go up after so many years of dealing with assholes who think I can't do anything simply because I have a vagina."

Even in the dim light, she saw his pupils flash. "Considering my head of security is female, and I respect the hell out of Cris, you should know by now that I'd never dismiss a female's capabilities."

"I do, Wes. It's just…habit. Probably like you using your dominance on me. So how about a sort of truce? Let's be equals. Agree to that, and I'll stay a few days on PineRock, and we can bounce strategies off one another."

She motioned for him to turn into the apartment complex and told him where to park. Once he did, Wes finally angled his torso toward her. His pupils flashed quickly as he answered, "Equals, but only once we reach PineRock. I'm going to be an overprotective bastard until we do."

She snorted. "I wouldn't expect anything less." Ashley gestured toward her apartment on the second floor. "I'll go pack some things right now, and we can head to PineRock tonight provided you promise to do the driving."

He grunted his approval before exiting the car. She followed suit.

As they made their way toward her place, she openly watched Wes check every dark corner for enemies, pausing at the slightest sound. Seeing him in his element, unlike back in the casino and bar, made him even more attractive to her. For crying out loud, she couldn't stop staring at his broad shoulders and trim hips like some starstruck teenager.

Get a grip, Ash. She'd never been around him for more than a day before. The next handful of days were going to test her in all sorts of ways. However, she'd have to pass any and all tests because failing would cause too much pain and suffering for the dragon clans in the area.

And after everything she'd worked toward, she wasn't about to let that happen.

As Wes drove the last few miles to PineRock, he kept glancing over to Ashley's sleeping face in the passenger seat.

He could hardly believe his female was going to be staying on PineRock. True, they had a mountain of problems to wade through, but it also gave him hope.

Hope that maybe, just maybe, they could find a path where they both kept protecting dragon-shifters while also snagging a small bit of happiness.

Because he was determined to make Ashley happy.

And also himself.

His dragon spoke up. *My, my, look who's singing a different tune now.*

The human men all but threatening Ashley had made Wes realize a few things about what was important. *If there's anyone who can find a way for an ADDA employee and a dragon-shifter to have a chance together while not losing their jobs, it's Ashley.*

His beast snorted. *That's the only reason you changed your mind, hmm? It has nothing to do with her heated looks or short dress tonight?*

He mentally growled. *Of course she's fucking beautiful. What do you expect, for me to say she's hideous?*

Now, now, calm down. I'm on your side.

Are you sure about that?

Ignoring his beast, Wes made the final turn toward the road that led to PineRock's main entrance. He only paused the car at the keypad checkpoint to enter the security code. Once the gates opened, he drove slowly through the tunnel carved into rock and out into the main area of his clan.

Even in the dark, a sense of peace came over him at the familiar streetlights, the odd house with a light in the window, and the quietness apart from some nocturnal animals brave enough to venture near PineRock.

He was home. He glanced at Ashley and mentally vowed she would never be harmed on his land. PineRock was the one place he possessed complete control, as well as the resources to make that promise a reality.

Wes drove a few minutes longer before he parked in front of a two-story house painted light green with beige trim. Even though he could've repaired it, he still spotted the claw marks in the siding from his early years of shifting into a dragon, when he'd thought to try jumping from the roof before he'd had lessons on how to fly.

He'd ended up at the clinic with a fractured wing.

His mother said those marks would stay until she was no longer around, as a reminder to him that not even Wes was invincible.

A light switched on in a window on the second story —his mother's room. He didn't want to wake her up, but Ashley needed to stay with someone he trusted. Well, someone he trusted and thought would be a little welcoming and not swamped with clan duties.

He said, "Ash, wake up."

His human merely grunted and went back to softly snoring.

It seemed she didn't wake easily. Yet another reason Ashley needed to stay on PineRock, in case someone tried to attack her while she was sleeping.

Time to try another tactic.

Wes risked touching her cheek with his fingers and resisted sucking in a breath at her soft, smooth skin. What he wouldn't give to wake her up with a kiss.

However, he wasn't going to kick off a mate-claim frenzy. So he lightly poked her cheek. "Wake up, sleepyhead."

"Why?" she muttered, her eyes still closed.

He poked a few more times, but she didn't do more than swat him away. So he resorted to some more extreme measures and tickled his fingers against her side.

She jumped and wiggled as she battled a frown with laughter. When he finally stopped, she glared at him. "What the hell, Wes? You could've just asked me to wake up."

"I did, and poked you, too. But it was almost like you were under some kind of sleep enchantment. If tickling hadn't worked, I might've had to dunk you in the lake."

Her brows came together. "I didn't wake up?" He shook his head, and she continued, "That's odd. I'm usually a light sleeper."

His dragon hummed. *She trusts us. That's good.*

While his human half was also pleased, Wes ignored the feeling. If he didn't act a little more in control when he introduced Ashley to his mom, who knew what sort of ideas his mother would come up with.

His dragon muttered, *She probably knows the truth anyway. Mom knows everything.*

He spoke to Ashley again. "I know you're tired, but I need you to stay awake a little longer. We're on PineRock, and I've brought you to my mom's house."

Her gaze took in the house dimly lit by a porch light. "Your mother's house?"

He nodded. "You'll stay with her for the next few days. And no, she doesn't know about what I told you tonight—I'm keeping it vague since dragons can hear more than you want to know—so don't worry about it.

She'll just be pleased to have someone stay with her. She's been alone ever since my younger brother joined the dragon unit of the Air Force last year."

Ashley rubbed the lingering traces of sleep from her eyes. "Please tell me she's not super chatty and a night owl. I'm so tired right now, and if I don't get some sleep, my brain won't work well enough to start tackling our mountain of problems in the morning."

He smiled at the slight frown on Ashley's face. He loved seeing her more vulnerable side. He replied, "I'll tell her to let you sleep tonight, but I can't make any promises about breakfast time."

His mother didn't much care for being alone but had refused to even think about another mate since Wes's dad had died.

She was lonely, and Ashley staying with her would be good all around.

The front door opened and his mother's voice drifted out. "Come out right now, Wesley Dalton, and tell me why you're here in the middle of the night."

Ashley laughed, not that he could blame her. His mother wore a fuzzy, bright pink bathrobe that was four sizes too big. But his mom liked to be warm and didn't care about how silly she looked.

Of course, on her short-for-a-dragon-shifter's frame, it made her look like a teenager. Albeit one with graying hair, but still not a middle-aged former dragon soldier.

Ashley managed to control her laughter. "Sorry, but I was expecting a much taller or intimidating woman to emerge. For some reason, that's what I picture when it comes to a clan leader's parents."

"Oh, don't let appearances fool you." His human shot him a curious look, but he ignored it and opened the car door. "Come on, or she'll drag us out by force. And that's not an exaggeration."

He exited the car and Ashley followed. Wes kissed his mother's cheek and murmured for her ears only, "I'm going to take her to the spare bedroom straight away. She's tired and needs some sleep. You can begin your interrogations tomorrow."

Her pupils flashed before she nodded. "I can sense something's wrong. I'll leave it for tonight, but you'd better tell me what's going on tomorrow. I can't look after a guest if I don't know the threats."

Few would believe it, but his mother had been in the Dragon Army Reserves before finding her mate. She had, in fact, been quite the intimidating female at one point.

He bobbed his head. "I'll share what I can, like always. Thanks in advance for your help, Mom."

She touched his cheek. "Anything for my eldest boy."

Ashley shuffled her feet, and Wes reached out to take her hand. "Ashley Swift, this is my mother, Cynthia Dalton. She's agreed to put off questions until the morning. So, come on. I'll show you to your room."

Ashley met his mom's gaze. "Nice to meet you, Mrs. Dalton."

"Call me Cynthia, please. And just know that we'll be

having breakfast together tomorrow morning—all three of us—so don't make any plans."

Wes knew better than to argue with his mother. "Fine, I'll be here at eight. Now, let me get Ashley to bed."

Without another word, he tugged his human upstairs and down the hall to the guest room. The fact it used to be his room when he was younger made both man and beast happy. Their female would be sleeping in the same room.

However, he didn't trust himself to be alone in the room with Ashley. So once he gently pushed her inside, he said, "There's a bathroom the next door down on the right stocked with just about anything you need. You already have my cell phone number, in case you need to call me. I'll keep it on, just in case. I'll see you tomorrow at breakfast."

With that, he shut the door and raced down the stairs. Wes somehow managed to wave to his mother and get away without another word, too.

As he headed back to his cottage, his dragon said, *Breakfast will be fun.*

Don't get too comfortable, dragon. Remember, there are still enemies out there.

There will always be enemies. However, I'm going to enjoy our breakfast with Ashley and Mom. It'll help us relax.

Relax? How in the hell is that possible when you'll be only thinking of claiming her?

His beast stood a little taller. *I can restrain myself. You'll see.*

Wes resisted sighing. He hoped so because dealing with both his dragon and his mother at the same time would be exhausting.

Still, it was basically a dream to have Ashely on Pine-Rock, staying in his old family home.

Not that he could linger on that thought. There was too much to do, and he needed to start on his clan leader duties ASAP. He changed the subject with his dragon. *For now, we need to send messages to Cris and Troy about what's going on. There's a lot to do before sunrise.*

Cris was in charge of clan security, and Troy was PineRock's head doctor. The pair were his closest confidants, and he'd long ago agreed to tell them everything when it came to the clan as a whole.

They were also two of the few clan members who knew that Ashley was Wes's true mate.

Walking faster, he soon reached his office. And as Wes went to work, the familiarity of clan business kept his mind from straying about having breakfast with his true mate.

Well, mostly. Wes had little control over his dreams, which had her in his house, naked, and at his mercy.

Chapter Six

The next morning, after Ashley had showered, changed, and did as much work on her phone as she could, she finally faced the door.

It was nearly 8:00 a.m., and she could hear Wes's mother moving around downstairs.

She was about to have breakfast with two dragon-shifters. The idea was kind of surreal given that ADDA had strict rules about how employees could interact with their charges. True, Wes wasn't exactly her charge, but he was close enough.

Even without ADDA rules and restrictions, there was a huge elephant in the room she still needed to discuss, too—being his true mate.

A night's sleep hadn't helped to settle her brain on that topic at all. If anything, sleep had made it worse since being near Wes for hours, inhaling his scent and feeling his heat, had only given her brain more fodder to use in her dream fantasies.

While there was plenty she didn't know about him, bidding on him and winning him for an evening may have not been the best idea. Because now she wanted more of everything—his touch, his teasing, and the feeling of being safe any time she was around him. All things she'd never felt with any other man.

Her cell phone beeped a reminder about the time, and she pushed aside every thought of a future with Wes. Figuring out what to do about the League was far more important. And to work on that issue, she needed to survive breakfast first.

So she stopped hesitating, opened the door, and headed down the stairs.

Despite not knowing the layout of the house, it was easy to follow the music and clanging to the kitchen. Ashley stopped in the doorway and smiled as she watched Cynthia do a little twirl before breaking an egg into a bowl.

The dragonwoman said without looking up, "Come in, Ashley. Breakfast will be ready soon-ish."

"Thank you," she murmured as she headed toward the tall chairs at the counter overhang.

Stirring the contents of the large bowl, Cynthia looked up. "I've seen you around and know you're an ADDA employee, but I'm not entirely sure how you ended up on PineRock in the middle of the night with my son."

Ashley did her best not to swing her feet as she thought of how to answer the question. In general, she didn't get along with a lot of women because she was too direct and wasn't very good at being delicate.

However, she'd just have to trust her gut, which said Cynthia wouldn't be offended at her being blunt despite the fact they'd just met. "I won him for the evening in a charity auction, but our night got cut short by the League."

Cynthia clicked her tongue. "The AHOLs, huh? I thought they'd mostly faded away around this part of the country."

She resisted blinking. It seemed Wes's mother was more informed than most of her fellow ADDA employees on the topic. "Er, yes, they were barely a flicker around here until a few years ago, when certain groups started funding recruitment drives again."

Cynthia poured some batter into a frying pan, picked up a spatula, and looked Ashley dead in the eye. "Then if Wes brought you here, in the middle of the night no less, it means you're in trouble. I hope you aren't one of those stupid females who think they can do everything without any help, even when it means facing people who probably want to kill you."

She snorted. Nope, Cynthia didn't mind bluntness, that was for sure. "I may be independent, but I'm not one of those ladies in the horror movie, the one who hears a noise and thinks, 'Oh, right, let's go check that out in my nightgown and slippers and ignore any shred of common sense.' I'd be the one calling for backup and staying inside with a baseball bat. I like the option with the greatest chance of success."

Cynthia nodded. "Good. Because my son doesn't need an imbecile for his true mate."

Ashley blinked. "Wait, what? I thought you didn't know about that."

"I'm his mother. Of course I know." Her tone softened and she smiled. "From all the interactions I've heard about you two, you'll be good for him. Sometimes a stubborn person needs another stubborn person to be persuaded of anything."

Oh, no, no, no. If Ashley wasn't careful, Wes's mom might try her hand at matchmaking. "Look, Cynthia...I can't have a future with Wes. Sorry, but my work with ADDA is important, and I'd have to give it up to live here."

The dragonwoman waved a hand in dismissal. "Of course your work is important. I'm not debating that. However, through the grapevine, I've heard of ADDA employees mating dragon-shifters and keeping their positions. It all depends on where you are, how the local ADDA office reacts, and what loophole you use. And before you ask, I don't know what the loopholes are. But if you want to stay on PineRock, there is probably a way to do it."

Ashley's mind buzzed. Just when she thought she

knew more about the American Department of Dragon Affairs than most, she was thrown a curveball.

Loopholes existed, apparently, and more than the mere niggling she'd had about clan leaders in good standing—which she still hadn't been able to recall. However, if she found one, would she stay with Wes?

As her mind screamed yes, the man in question appeared in the doorway. Ashley blinked at his appearance.

She'd thought him sexy in his clothes from the night before, but even though he wore a simple T-shirt and jeans, his wet, tossed hair and cleanly shaven face made her speechless.

As he snatched up a few grapes from the bowl on the counter and popped them into his mouth, his biceps bulging in all the right places, she instantly felt the need to jump into his arms and kiss him.

She frowned. No, that was ridiculous. She simply didn't jump men and kiss them because they looked sexy.

Wes swallowed before grinning at his mother. "You made your special pancakes, I see."

His grin made her lady parts sigh with wanting.

Damn the man.

Cynthia pointed her spatula at Wes. "I did, but you'll wait your turn. The guest gets fed first."

Wes pushed the bowl of grapes toward her. "Here, Ash. Eat something."

She was about to thank him when his mother

snorted. "And no, giving her a few grapes doesn't count as feeding her first."

"Damn," he muttered with a wink.

Unable to help herself, Ashley pelted him with a grape. "I know the way to a man's stomach is food, but you're clearly not starving and in excellent shape."

He leaned over and whispered into her ear, "You noticed what shape I'm in, huh?"

She searched his gaze. "Who are you and what have you done with Wes Dalton?"

Tucking a section of hair behind her ear—his touch making her shiver—he murmured, "You'll see soon enough when we can talk in private."

A mixture of both excitement and caution danced through her body. "And when will that be?"

He straightened up, took the plate full of food from his mother, and placed it in front of her. "After breakfast. Now, eat."

Normally she'd remark on his order, but her stomach rumbled, and she looked down.

What she saw on her plate was almost like a piece of art. Somehow, Cynthia had made a cartoony dragon head, complete with eyes and nostril slits made out of blueberries and raisins. "It's too cute to eat."

"Nonsense," Cynthia stated. "I've been making these since Wes was three years old, back when he refused to eat much of anything. I could make five hundred more in my sleep. So dig in, Ashley. And quickly, before Wes tries to steal your food."

"I wouldn't steal it," Wes grumbled.

Ashley couldn't help it, she laughed. However, she quickly sobered as a realization hit her, and she said out loud, "The dragons I've visited over the years have really been holding back their true selves, haven't they?"

Wes sat next to her. "Don't take it personally. It's hard enough to be told what you can and can't do on a constant basis. I think some are afraid that if you know how much we treasure our clan and family, ADDA will find a way to break it apart to control us further."

She shook her head. "Not all of us are like that."

"But enough of you are."

Ashley couldn't argue with him. For the first seven of her ten years working with ADDA, all her superiors had been hell-bent on reminding the dragon-shifters that they were second-class citizens.

It was only with the promotion of Steven Greenwood to the Southwestern ADDA office, and his belief that trust and understanding was more effective long-term than fear, had Ashley been allowed to do more than bark orders and cite regulations.

To be honest, she had nearly reached a place where she'd wanted to quit ADDA. But Greenwood's attitude had inspired her to try harder, to the point she'd been put in charge of the dragon lotteries in the area.

Wes touched her shoulder. "Hey, you're not that bad. True, sometimes you try to order me around and remind me that you're my superior, but it's mostly done when I'm being a stubborn ass myself."

Some of the time, but not all. However, she didn't want to bring down the mood, so she replied, "I'm just glad you started telling me to back off sometimes. It most definitely made my job more fun."

He lowered his voice dramatically. "Don't tell anyone, but it made it fun for me, too. To the point I made a list of new ways to irritate you on purpose."

She leaned her face on her hand. "Now I'm curious about this list of yours."

Wes ate a few grapes before replying, "Let's deal with the League first, and then we'll see if you earn enough points to see my list."

She raised her brows. "Earn enough points? What am I, some sort of student or reality show contestant now?"

Cynthia jumped in. "Let her eat, Wes. You two can have your verbal sparring session later."

She half-expected for Wes to tell his mother to mind her own business. However, he chuckled and moved to help her finish cooking the remaining pancakes. He said over his shoulder, "I'll do a little supervising and taste testing over here. Otherwise my mother will try to feed you twenty pancakes, like you're a dragon-shifter."

As Wes and his mother traded a few barbs with love, she smiled. Ashley had lost her mother a number of years ago and missed her dearly. Maybe if, and that was a big if, she could stay and be Wes's mate and still do her ADDA work, Cynthia could help fill the emptiness in her heart.

Not that she should be making any sort of long-term plans like that. *Focus on the League, Swift.* And with that thought, she ate her pancakes and tried to think of solutions to discuss with Wes. Talks of the future—any future —would need to wait a little while longer.

Chapter Seven

Wes usually enjoyed his mother's teasing and penchant for talking. However, as his mother regaled some tale about how her younger brother was sneaking off the clan's land to meet a human—something he'd have to check into later—he couldn't stop stealing glances at Ashley.

Watching the female eat in her borrowed nightshirt and barely tamed morning hair did something to both man and beast.

His dragon spoke up. *Because she should look that way in our bed, not in our mom's kitchen. Except when she's there, she'll be naked.*

We discussed this at length last night. Give me a little time before trying to convince her to be naked in our bed.

Fine, but don't wait too long, or I may try to take control for a while.

The threat was mostly just talk since his beast would

never try to harm or coerce their fated female. However, it wasn't as if Wes wanted to hold back around Ashley for longer than possible, either.

He'd decided last night that he would give in to his desires and fight for her. And once he made up his mind regarding something so important, it wasn't easily swayed.

Even if he had to move mountains or force a change in ADDA policy so she could be happy, Ashley Swift would be his mate.

His mother poked his side and whispered so softly that a human wouldn't be able to hear her. "I'll be having a daughter-in-law soon, won't I?"

It didn't surprise him that his mother would've picked up on his interest. He answered in the same hushed tones, "If it's at all possible, yes. But don't meddle in this, Mom. I can handle it."

"We'll see, Wes. We'll see." She held out a plate stacked with pancakes. "Now, go eat with her so you two can talk."

Since reminding his mother that he could make his own decisions was pointless most of the time—and only wasted energy—he slid into the seat next to Ashley. When his leg brushed hers, electricity raced up his thigh and straight to his cock.

Her fork paused halfway to her mouth and she met his gaze.

His human had felt it too.

His beast hummed. *Yes, of course she did. Do it again.*

Not wanting to encourage his beast, he cleared his throat and said, "We'll have a little time to talk alone once you've finished eating. However, full-on talks of solutions will have to wait because you have an appointment to train with Ryan and one of the Protectors later this morning."

Ryan Ford was a human who had mated Gaby Santos, a dragonwoman on PineRock. After being dropped from a great height and barely caught before reaching the ground—which had caused damage to his spine—the recovery had been a long one for the male. However, Ryan was training again and would have some good pointers for Ashley about how the hell a human could defend themselves against a dragon-shifter, which should mostly work against stronger opponents in general.

And since Ryan was mated, in love, and about to become a father, Wes's dragon didn't mind Ashley spending time alone with him.

Ashley replied, "I've always wondered about his and Tori's training sessions. I guess it can't hurt, although I hope it'll be effective against humans as well since I don't think I have any dragon-shifter enemies."

He sat up a little taller and stated, "PineRock is safe for humans now." It'd taken months to clean out those who had tried to hurt the humans, Tori and Ryan, but he'd done it. "But yes, it'll be good against any opponent stronger than you. I'd train you myself, but I have some clan duties I have to deal with first."

She tilted her head. "Ones I can't watch? I've always wondered about what you do all day. Okay, I wonder about all dragon leaders, but maybe a little more about you."

The fact Ashley was interested in his work was yet another sign of how right she was for him. Especially since she knew it wasn't all glory and adulation—it involved a shit-ton of paperwork.

Even though he wanted to share everything with her, he shook his head. "No, you can't shadow me this morning. I trust you, but not everyone does yet, and your presence could make some people hold back when they really shouldn't. Just give it some time, okay?" Even though he should avoid touching her until they were alone, Wes took her free hand and squeezed it gently. "Soon enough they'll see what I see."

For a few beats, they merely stared at one another. Damn, his human was so beautiful with her blue eyes and dark hair.

Throw in the fact she was smart as hell and full of fire, and the urge to carry her off to his house and kiss her surged.

No. He couldn't allow the clan to be unprotected or unprepared. When, not if Wes had his mate-claim frenzy, he'd know his clan was ready for his absence for a few weeks.

His dragon spoke up. *Then start working on that today, too. Because the second she signals she wants us and we can claim her without putting people in danger, I'm going to do it.*

Ashley gripped his hand a little tighter, bringing him back to their conversation. "Shadowing you will be the first thing I add to my list of things you'll show me later."

He raised his brows. "Now I have a list?"

She smiled, and he stopped breathing a second. How he'd resisted her for so long, he had no idea.

Somehow he caught her reply, "It seemed only fair since you have a list for me." She leaned an inch closer, her scent even stronger. "Although I'll make sure you carry out each item on my list. I'm hoping you won't go to extreme lengths to irritate me, though."

"Ah, but you see, it's fun to see your cheeks flush and eyes fill with fire. So I'm not sure you'll be successful with changing my mind there."

She whispered, "We'll see about that."

If not for his mother in the same room, he might've tried inching his free hand between her legs. He could smell her arousal and didn't think she'd say no.

However, his mother *was* there. What had been a smart idea to keep them acting like adults without their hormones getting in the way had turned into a nuisance.

Ashley was too tempting by half.

His dragon spoke up. *Then let her eat so we can talk with her in private. Maybe then she'll let you kiss her skin, or maybe even more.*

No mate-claim frenzies yet, dragon.

There's a lot you can do without starting one.

Not only was that true, but Wes was one of a handful who knew that dragon-shifters could have sex with their

71

true mates and not kick off the mate-claim frenzy. Provided, of course, they could avoid kissing on the lips.

Not that Wes would claim his mate fully until he could kiss her, too.

Although savoring the sweet honey between her thighs was most definitely on the table.

With every bit of willpower he possessed, he released her hand and scooted her plate toward her a little more. "Finish eating, Ash. Quickly."

And given how she did so without the least bit of resistance at his order told him that she was just as eager to be alone with him, too.

Shoveling what was left of his food into his mouth, he sat and watched his human. There was so much he burned to know about her—from the little things of what she preferred to drink to the bigger things such as how she'd act in his bed—but he settled for the domesticity of watching her eat.

He wouldn't rush her, but he hoped like hell she'd finish soon. He wanted to claim every minute before her training session and make the most of it.

ASHLEY FELT Wes's gaze the entire time she ate, but she still didn't eat any less than normal.

Sure, her stomach had a few butterflies, but she was hungry. And she wasn't going to set the tone that a glare or intense gaze from Wes would make her change course.

One of the benefits of working with dragon-shifters for so long was that she understood the dominance scale better than most humans. And while she didn't want to be on the top, above him, she wanted equal footing.

Well, for most things. The thought of him holding her wrists above her head in bed as he thrust hard into her pussy made her a little wet.

Stop it, Swift. He'll notice.

Peeking from the corner of her eye, she noted his intense, smoldering gaze hadn't altered. Not even his pupils were flashing. Maybe he hadn't noticed.

Once she was full and swilled some water around her mouth—she was grateful that she'd brushed her teeth already to banish her morning breath—she turned toward Wes with a smile.

This time, his pupils flashed between round and slitted. Some might run at the sight, but it only made her nipples tighten harder.

Being the focus of a dragon-shifter could be heady stuff.

Clearing her throat, she forced her gaze to Cynthia. "Thanks for breakfast. It was delicious."

"You're welcome. I expect you back for dinner tonight. Make sure it happens, okay, Wes?"

Wes grunted, and his mother added, "Now, go and hash out some things. As it stands now, I could use a knife to cut the tension between you two."

Even though all of Wes's stares hadn't made her

blush recently, her cheeks heated at his mother's comment.

If she noticed the attraction sizzling between them, how in the world were they supposed to keep it from everyone else until they were ready?

And yep, she'd just all but admitted to herself that one day, she wanted everyone to know about her and the dragon leader.

Wes put out a hand. "Come on."

Not trusting her voice, Ashley placed her hand in his. The second skin met skin, she barely registered his heat before Wes tugged her out of the kitchen and toward a rear sliding door in the living room. "Where are we going? I'm not even dressed."

"Don't worry. I have a secret pathway between my place and my mom's, one where no one can see us without using a ladder or flying overhead."

As he unlocked the slider, she sighed. "That still doesn't address me not having shoes, let alone pants on."

Once the door was open, he turned toward her, his pupils flashing. "I'm going to carry you."

Before she could do more than open her mouth, Wes swept her into his arms. The second she crashed against his hard, warm chest, her entire body instantly molded to his form.

Damn the man. Even when she should put up a protest, her body had its own ideas.

Determined to at least have some control in the situation, she growled. "You're supposed to ask my permission before just carrying me around."

He raised his brows. "Would you rather walk on the cold ground?"

True, it was early spring, which wasn't exactly warm in the greater Tahoe area. "Of course not. But your chivalry has a massive flaw—I don't even have a coat on, which is even worse."

He held her closer against his body. "I'll keep you warm."

With any other man, she'd roll her eyes. However, Wes radiated delicious heat to the point she inadvertently snuggled against him.

His chuckle rolled over her. "I think you agree."

She muttered, "I still like to be asked."

"Next time, I will." He kissed her forehead, and her heart skipped a beat. His firm yet soft lips against her skin made her belly flip and her core pulse.

What would happen when he actually kissed her on the lips?

Reminded of being his true mate at that, she found her voice again. "Fine. Then you'd better run before I freeze to death."

The corner of his mouth ticked up. "Just remember —you asked for it."

He stepped out, shut the door, and dashed down a pathway with tall hedges on either side.

Not that she could tell more than that they were hedges since everything became blurry super quickly.

As the wind chilled her skin, she leaned more into Wes, which he took as his cue to hold her even closer against his chest. His speed picked up even more until they soon reached another house and entered before she could tell more than it was a dark brown color.

Not even out of breath, Wes shut the door and asked, "Was that fast enough?"

She snorted. "Maybe. I'm sure you're even faster in your dragon form."

His pupils flashed a few times before he replied, "Don't encourage my beast. Now he'll think of nothing but shifting so he can show off."

Ashley had seen Wes's dragon once before and only remembered he was a black dragon. "Maybe he can come out later. I never really got a chance to study your dragon up close and personal."

Wes's pupils turned slitted a few beats before returning to round. "Great, now I'll have to keep negotiating to stay human for the foreseeable future."

He slid her down his body, and whatever retort she had on her lips was forgotten.

As soon as she was on her feet, she instinctively leaned against him. Wes wrapped his arms around her and whispered, "Let me warm you up, and then we'll talk."

Her body was already on fire thanks to being surrounded by a tall, muscled dragonman, but she merely nodded and leaned her head on his shoulder.

While he could no doubt feel the hard points of her

nipples and smell her arousal, Ashley didn't care. Right here, right now, she was surrounded in heat, security, and something else she couldn't quite define.

She wondered how the hell she'd resisted him for all these years.

Wes finally broke the silence. "I wish I could hold you all day, but you know I can't. If you want to talk, we need to do it soon."

Hugging him close a second longer, she reveled in the mixture of feelings he provoked before raising her head. "Okay, so let's talk, starting with the complete change in your demeanor. Why is that?"

He shrugged one shoulder. "I decided to stop fighting it. I want you as my mate, Ashley Swift. And I'm willing to do whatever it takes to make it happen."

Chapter Eight

Maybe Wes should've eased into his declaration of intent, but he had a limited amount of time to spend with his female and didn't want to waste it.

If she also wanted him, then only part of their time together this morning would be about talking.

His dragon grunted. *I say less talking and more kissing, licking and lapping.*

Ignoring his beast, Wes waited for Ashley's response to his statement.

She searched his eyes for about thirty seconds before replying, "Maybe it's crazy to say this, but I think I'd like being your mate, Wes. However, there's a lot to do before that can happen."

His beast roared in excitement. Wes cupped Ashley's cheek and said, "I know there is. But I want to make doubly sure about this, Ash. Because dragons grow extremely attached to their mates, as you well know. And

I won't be able to just change my mind in a few hours if you get cold feet."

Fire flashed in her eyes and relieved his uneasiness a fraction. "I've known you for years. Hell, I ended my engagement because I realized it would be wrong to marry anyone else when I was still constantly dreaming of you. So instead, I just resigned myself to a life of wanting someone I could never have." She gripped his shirt and tugged gently. "So if I say I want you, I mean it. All I need is your promise that we do two things—one, find a way for me to still help dragonkind and two, you keep your alpha possessiveness in front of others mostly in check until we do."

Tell her yes. Hurry, hurry. Then we can at least taste her skin. Maybe even her pussy.

Stroking his thumb against her cheek, he answered, "I can agree to that." Wes leaned even closer. "And I think it's time to celebrate a little."

He heard Ashley's heart beat even faster. "I already know you're strong in more than just the physical sense since you've resisted me for so long. But what, er, kind of celebrations can you do without going over the edge?"

He took a second to nuzzle her cheek, both man and beast nearly groaning. Wes had dreamed of doing this, and so much more, for so long. And it looked like he was about to start making his dreams come true.

When Ashley's nails dug into his chest as a small moan escaped her lips, he smiled and answered, "I can't kiss you on the lips until we know for sure everything is safe and figured out, but let me show you just a fraction of how much I want you. Will you let me, Ash?"

Her lips brushed his jaw and Wes groaned. Her husky voice whispered into his ear, "As long as I get to show you, too."

Unable to hold back any longer, Wes leaned back and tore off her shirt. Ashley gasped but then arched her back, putting her beautiful breasts on display. Accepting the invitation, he leaned down and licked one taut bud and then the other.

When her nails dug into the back of his head and tried to move it downward, his cock turned to stone. She said, "Kiss me everywhere else you can, Wes. But hurry, because I want a turn, too."

For a split second, Wes thought he was dreaming. But then her nails dug in harder and reminded him that this was no dream.

Ashley Swift, his true mate, was naked except for her underwear, all but begging him to play with her nipples.

And hinting she wanted to suck his cock.

His dragon roared. *Stop thinking and wondering. Just do it already.*

With a growl, Wes took one of her firm nipples between his lips and suckled. Hard.

Ashley cried out, the scent of her arousal growing stronger.

Unable to resist, he ran a hand down her belly and cupped her pussy over her underwear.

Releasing her tit with a pop, he murmured, "I think

there's another part of you aching, no, burning for my lips, my tongue, my teeth. Am I right?"

"Yes," she breathed.

He rubbed the palm of his hand against her clit, loving how she moved with him. His voice was husky as he said, "Say you want me to lick that pussy like there's no tomorrow, until you scream my name and explode on my tongue."

Some females might tense or grow cold at his dirty talk, but not his human. She reached a hand down, pushed his away, and then pulled aside the crotch of her panties. "Please, Wes. I've been wet for you for years. Touch me."

Not needing another reminder, he kneeled, tore off her underwear, and slowly pushed her back against the wall. Hitching one of her legs over his shoulder, his mouth watered at her dripping pussy.

He ran a finger through her center, his cock letting out a drop of precum at how wet she was. For him.

His beast grunted. *Hurry and taste her, lick her. Let her know how much we want her.*

Soon. But first, I'm going to torture her a little.

Wes lightly pushed his finger inside her, and Ashley arched her back as she blurted, "I wish it was your cock, Wes."

So it seemed his human was a little dirty when naked. She was too fucking perfect for him. "Soon, Ash. But not today."

She whimpered, and he nearly risked turning her around and taking her from behind.

But somehow, Wes restrained himself. Not until he made her orgasm from his tongue would he put his cock anywhere near her pussy.

Using her own wetness, he swirled around her hard, little clit, loving how her hips bucked, almost as if trying to make him touch her where she ached.

Removing his finger, he finally lowered his head and lightly flitted his tongue against her hard bud.

"Wes! Oh, god, please. Harder."

Not ready for her to come just yet, he kept his tongue light, swirling her clit before heading down to her center. He lightly thrust inside her a few times, groaning at her sweet taste. He finally couldn't help but whisper, "You're so fucking perfect. I could eat you all day."

She tugged his hair once before pressing him toward her. "Later. You can take your time later. Please, Wes. Finger me as you make me come."

His beast hummed in approval, but Wes didn't pay him any attention. His mouth descended on her tight bud as he pressed one finger inside her. She was so wet, and hot, and tight.

Fuck, he wanted to feel her heat around his cock.

Since that wouldn't happen right now, he suckled her clit as he added a second finger. As he thrust his hand, he licked, swirled, and even bit her clit until Ashley was breathing hard and about to draw blood from how her nails dug into his scalp.

He thrust hard one last time as he bit a little harder. Ashley screamed as she spasmed around his fingers.

Needing to taste her orgasm, he removed his fingers and replaced them with his tongue, moaning at the taste of her sweet nectar, loving how she gripped him as if she never wanted to let go.

He could do this a thousand times, and he'd never get tired of her.

When she finally relaxed against the wall, Wes removed his tongue and looked up at her, loving her flushed cheeks and heavy breathing.

He quickly unzipped his jeans and took out his cock. Stroking it, he moved to tease her pussy again with his mouth. Once was most definitely not enough.

However, Ashley took his chin in her hand and tilted his gaze upward. "No," she stated.

For a second, he wondered if she'd regretted what they'd just done. But then she smiled slowly and licked her lips. "It's my turn."

He nearly came right then and there but squeezed the head of his cock to tame it back.

Ashley said, "Stand up."

And Wes could do nothing but obey, eager for one of his most desired fantasies to come true.

Ashley had never been so confident with a man before, but there was something about Wes that made her bold, demanding, and honest.

And more attracted to someone than she'd ever been in her life.

As her orgasm haze faded, she wanted nothing more than to give him the same as she'd gotten. Not just because it was owed, or some other such bullshit. No, she actually craved to taste Wes and have him at her mercy for a short while.

He didn't say no when she said she wanted a turn, and he stood up with his hand still around his dick. She stared at his flashing dragon eyes a few beats before lowering to her knees.

And even then, Wes kept his hand clenched over the head of his cock. She placed her hand over his and murmured, "Let go and show me."

He did, revealing the long, hard shaft jutting out from his body. She'd heard rumors of dragon-shifters being well-endowed, but Wes was long and thick, and she swore she saw his dick twitch the longer she stared at it.

Wes's strained voice garnered her attention. "If you keep staring and licking your lips like that, Ash, I'm not going to last."

She hadn't even realized she'd been doing those things. "So I guess that rumor about a dragonman's stamina isn't true then?"

He growled. "Of course it fucking is. But I've wanted you for years, thought of how your sweet mouth would feel around me. And with your taste still on my tongue, it's all too much. After this first time to get it out of my system, I'm going to make it last until you beg for it."

She glanced upward. "I'll add that challenge to my list."

However, before Wes could say anything, she lightly ran her finger over the head of his dick, swirling the wetness there and barely noting Wes's quick intake of breath.

Ashley was far from a virgin, but never had a man nearly come from a mere touch of her fingers. She wondered how else she could work him up, as he'd done her.

She moved her hand to the base and gripped. Hard.

Wes's hand went to her head and pushed forward. "I've never begged before, but I'm about to do it if you don't hurry up."

She smiled. "No begging necessary."

Opening her mouth, she licked the tip once, twice, three times, loving how Wes thrust his hips slightly with each tease.

And while she'd think of ways to torture him longer, her core pulsed, eager to suck and taste him. He'd said she tasted better than anything he'd ever had, and she was curious if it was the same with him.

Not wanting her dragonman to wait any longer, she took him into her mouth and sucked lightly. Wes swore and gripped her hair in his hand. "Fuck, yes. Take me deeper, love. I want to feel more of you."

Even though she could never probably take all of him, she built up a rhythm, swallowing him a little deeper each time she moved her head back and forth.

Under her free hand against his thigh, she felt his muscles tremble, much like hers had. Except she wanted to push it further, so she reached below and cupped his balls.

Wes roared and thrust into her mouth. Soon the pair of them had a rhythm, and Ashley figured out how he liked his balls squeezed or how to twirl her tongue to make him moan.

There was something heady about having so much power over a man.

No, a dragonman. And she would make sure that no other woman would ever have this power over Wes again.

He was hers.

Unwilling to dwell on that realization, she moved faster, until Wes grunted out, "I'm going to come, love."

If he expected her to pull away, he would be sadly disappointed. The traces of his male musk had made her crave even more.

So when he finally stilled and exploded, Ashley swallowed every last drop.

Eventually, Wes pushed against her head, and she let him go, lingering a few beats to lick the tip one last time. He gently tugged her hair to make her look up, and she did. And for a second, she saw a mixture of the normal emotions a man had after an orgasm—lust, bliss, and contentment.

However, there was also a tenderness that made her want to stand up and hold him close.

So she stood and cupped his cheeks. Wes wrapped his arms around her and placed a possessive hand on her ass. He murmured, "That was better than any fucking fantasy, Ash. You are my dream made real."

Brushing her fingers against his jaw, she almost wished he had some stubble. "I think your dick is still doing the talking."

His pupils flashed, and he held her tighter against him. "No, I mean it. You are my perfect match in every way—from your fire to your stubbornness to your silly list and, most especially, your perfect little mouth. We may not have had our ceremony or made anything official, but to me, you're already my mate, Ashley Swift. No other female will ever compare."

The statement should scare her, or maybe irritate her a little at having no say, but for some reason, his words just felt right.

She wasn't sure if she could go back to her rainbow-filled apartment and try to carve out a life of solitude again. She yearned to be a part of something, to have a partner, to love and be loved.

And all of that she wanted to do with Wes.

Not just wanted—she *would* do it with him.

She finally replied, "I don't mind if you say things like that when we're alone, but not in public yet, okay? There's still the little matter of me staying here and finding a way to stay with ADDA so I can help dragon-shifters."

He stroked her back in slow circles, which made her lean even more against his hard chest. His voice rumbled, and the vibrations against her nipples made her want to sigh with longing. "That just means we have to work hard to find a solution soon. Because I don't want any other male to think he has a chance with you."

The corner of her mouth ticked up. "With me, the ADDA lady who barks orders and sets the rules? I don't think you'll have to worry about that."

"It attracted the hell out of me, so don't discount it so easily."

She sighed, kissed where his throat met his chest, and murmured, "I think I need to soothe your dragon ego again before I leave for training, to make sure you don't start growling at any man I come into contact with."

He tilted her head upward with his fingers. "There is a way you can do that and enjoy the process, I think."

"Oh?"

His pupils flashed a few times before he growled, "Let me make you scream two more times in the next twenty minutes. It'll make man, beast, and my female happy."

Just the thought of Wes licking her pussy or teasing her clit made wetness rush between her legs again. "I want to say yes, but maybe we should try to get some actual work done?"

He lifted her against him until she had to wrap her

legs around his waist. His cock was still hard and currently nestled against her clit.

So close, and yet so far.

After moving to her ear, he whispered, "Challenge accepted, then. I'll make you scream twice in ten minutes, and then we can have a little time to discuss work and the future."

Before she could say yes or no, Wes moved into the living room, set her on the back of the couch, and knelt between her thighs.

Ashley quickly forgot about anything but Wes's tongue, fingers, and even a little bit of teasing with one of his talons.

Her dragonman knew how to distract her, that was for sure. That just meant Ashley would have to find a way to resist him.

But not quite yet. No, she wanted to be thoroughly distracted until she screamed his name twice more.

Chapter Nine

Two hours later, Ashley leaned over, bracing her arms against her thighs, breathing heavily and trying not to think about how much she'd hurt the next morning. "How in the hell do you do that almost every day?"

Ryan Ford flashed a grin. "You just have to build up some stamina."

A woman's voice she recognized filled the air. "Which comes in handy for more than just training, by the way."

Standing fully upright, Ashley turned toward the dragonwoman named Gaby Santos-Ford and snorted. "I swear dragons only think about sex."

"Not only. But it definitely makes life a lot more fun." Gaby walked—or, more appropriately waddled as she was eight months pregnant—to her mate and leaned against Ryan. "Just don't kill her by mistake, okay, Ryan? I think Wes likes her."

It took every bit of Ashley's training not to show her emotions. While she rarely succeeded in hiding them anymore with Wes, her cheeks didn't color for Gaby or Ryan. "The pair of you should like me, too, considering how I coordinated the dragon lotteries and ultimately selected both of you to participate. Otherwise, you wouldn't be mated with a baby on the way, now, would you?"

Gaby chuckled. "No. But I'll admit I cursed you for a few years because of never picking my name for the lottery. However, in all seriousness, I don't think I've ever really thanked you. Because I never would've found Ryan otherwise."

As the pair stared at each other lovingly, each of them resting a hand over Gaby's protruding belly, a thread of jealousy shot through Ashley's body.

It shouldn't matter as she all but had Wes as her own. But Ryan and Gaby could be affectionate or hold each other, or tease without being scrutinized.

Unlike Ashley and Wes.

The sight of the loving couple only made Ashley more determined to find a loophole where she could keep her job to help the dragon-shifters as well as claim her man. And fast.

Speaking of which, she checked the time before heading toward her belongings off to the side of the large training room. "I'm supposed to meet Wes and then visit Tori, so I should be going."

Ryan replied, "So you'll be back tomorrow for more training?"

She picked up her purse, water bottle, and towel. "I'll try, but I won't know until tonight if I'll have the time. I'll let you know either way by text."

Ashley waved goodbye as she exited the room. However, after taking a few steps into the hall, someone grabbed her wrist. Looking up, she met the determined brown-eyed gaze of PineRock's head of security, Cris Juarez. Ashley frowned. "I didn't think I had a meeting with you."

"You didn't, but you do now. Stay quiet until we reach my office."

From her time working with the dragonwoman, Ashley knew better than to try and ask for more details until they did as she said.

Cris's brusque manner might seem disrespectful to some, but Ashley knew the dragonwoman had to keep up appearances for the sake of her clan. There weren't many female head Protectors in the US—at least that Ashley knew about—which meant Cris had to be extra careful about how she acted, or she'd be challenged by her male colleagues.

Maybe not from within the clan itself since they were loyal to Cris, but it wasn't completely unheard of for a nearby clan to try and apply for the head Protector position in the greater Tahoe area. There were four clans, and at one point, they'd changed hands repeatedly through constant challenges until an agreement had been reached a number of years ago.

Now, only extremely dire situations or a provable lack in abilities meant a challenge could be issued.

As Ashley thought of how she and Cris both had to put on acts to fit in with their male colleagues, they soon reached the main Protector building.

She barely paid attention to the tall, concrete building, having seen it hundreds of times before. As soon as Cris shut the door to her office on the second floor, the dragonwoman dropped Ashley's hand and said without preamble, "One of my Protectors noticed some unusual activity on the main road leading to PineRock. The short version is that some League assholes were snooping around a few of the trails nearby, almost as if they were trying to find a way to get here on foot."

So it seemed the confrontation the night before—had it only been then?—had already come back to bite her in the ass. "They'll be looking for me, no doubt."

Cris nodded. "My guy Andre overheard some of their conversation. The League guys were determined to find a less-obvious way to PineRock so they could rescue the humans here and make sure you didn't let any others come to stay."

Ashley raised her brows. "Well, considering how they didn't think you'd have sentries, or even try to monitor for threats, they seem low-risk to me, right?"

"Perhaps. But it's the first time League dumbasses have

come within ten miles of PineRock in over a decade. Since you're our ADDA contact, not to mention you have a vested interest in this place since you're friendly with Wes, I figured you needed to know ASAP. That way, you can work some of your magic and help the problem go away."

Considering Cris was excellent at keeping PineRock safe, it had to kill her to admit she needed Ashley's help. But it was true—ADDA dealt with the human enemy side of things. It was bureaucracy at its worst, considering how the dragons should be able to protect themselves.

But now wasn't the time to challenge the idea and rock the boat. Not if she wanted to mate Wes and still work with ADDA.

Ashley replied, "I need to talk with Wes first before I make any sort of call."

Crossing her arms in front of her, Cris pinned Ashley with a hard stare. "Tell me you aren't yanking him around, Swift. Only Troy and I know the full extent— that you're true mates—but Wes is more than my leader, he's my friend. And I won't let him be hurt, not even by the likes of someone I don't usually hate."

Anger flared in her chest. "Have I ever given you reason to think I'd hurt Wes, even before things changed? No. So I'll keep on trying to protect your clan, just as I've been doing for years."

After a beat, Cris smiled. "Good. I had to test you. I'm glad someone doesn't cower under the patented Juarez stare down."

Her mood lightened, and the corner of her mouth kicked up. "You only have to deal with one clan leader— I've dealt with more than a half a dozen. A backbone is sort of required."

Cris laughed. "Good." She gestured toward the door. "Wes is in his office down the hall. Just make sure you talk first and do all the touchy-feely stuff later."

Unable to help herself, Ashley flipped off Cris. "I'll somehow manage."

The two shared one last smile—Ashley liked the head Protector even more now—before she left and headed toward Wes's office. She rang the doorbell and waited for him to unlock the door to more than just his room. No, they were going to get serious about planning their future, which included dealing with the League idiots.

WES DID his best to focus on his computer, but he kept glancing at the door, hoping Ashley would show up.

If he weren't clan leader and didn't have over a thousand sets of eyes on him, he might've gone to her training session and brought her back to his office straightaway.

But that would be unusual behavior for a clan leader when it came to an ADDA employee, especially when only a few knew where he'd been last night and with whom.

Clan leaders usually didn't go running after ADDA employees if they could help it.

His dragon yawned. *It's just a few humans wandering in the woods. I wouldn't exactly call them huge threats.*

They represent a much bigger problem, though. If a movement rises, calling for the League to "liberate" all humans from the dragon clans, it could spell out war.

His beast didn't answer. Probably because they both knew that lately, anti-dragon sentiment had been on the rise again.

A few strategic ad campaigns and accompanying actions could stoke that fire to unbearable levels.

Just as he tried to focus back on the new agreement in front of him between a new human farm partner and PineRock, a patterned chime echoed inside the room.

He crossed to the door in seconds and checked the peephole.

The sight of Ashley staring at him only made Wes crave her presence more. Not just for the physical, but her mental might, as well.

So he opened the door, and as soon as Ashley was inside, he slammed it and pulled her close. Her comfortable heat, curves, and scent helped ease his anxiety a fraction.

She murmured, "Are things worse than what Cris told me?"

He nuzzled her cheek a few seconds before replying, "No, but I like knowing you're safe with me."

Ashley sighed. "I've been surrounded by Protectors ever since this morning. If you keep worrying about me walking a quarter of a mile, you're going to turn into a shitty leader real quick."

His human, blunt as ever.

With a chuckle, he met her gaze again. "I know. But until we're officially mated, I'm going to be a little on edge. I'd blame it on my dragon, but we're both just as eager to claim you with a ceremony in front of everyone."

She touched his cheek. Her soft fingers made his dragon hum in contentment. "Wes, it'll happen soon. But first, we need to deal with these idiots thinking to liberate, whatever the fuck that's supposed to mean, the humans here. Call me crazy, but I don't think Jose or Gaby are going to like the idea of their mates being carted away."

The sibling pair of Jose and Gaby were devoted to their human mates and more than a little possessive of them.

He gestured toward the loveseat off to the side. Only once they were both seated—Ashley close enough his thigh touched hers—did he elaborate on the situation. "Basically, there's little I can do myself. Under normal circumstances, you'd put in a call to the ADDA office, their police team would come to enforce the laws, and we could mostly ignore them. However, if the ADDA police show up and find the League guys, the human bastards could share our secret about last night. You'd be fired, and then half of the future you want would vanish." He took her hand in his. "So what other options are there? I'm open to any and all ideas."

Ashley tapped her chin. And while it was one of her habits to help her think—Wes had picked up on most of them over the years—he was impatient. Each tap only made him more so.

His dragon spoke up. *Stop acting so fucking irrational. You're better than this.*

Normally, yes. But this is our mate we're talking about. I don't understand how you're so calm.

Because Ashley is smart and doesn't put up with bullshit. Just give her a few minutes. It won't kill you.

Ashley's voice prevented him from replying to his beast. "I say keep an eye on them for a few days, long enough for us to investigate the possible loopholes your mother mentioned." Ashley explained what his mother had said the day before and added, "There's one I've been thinking about, too. Something to do with clan leaders in good standing. However, it might be quicker to reach out to any allies and see what they say. Surely you get along with at least one of the nearby clans? I know it's technically illegal to make formal alliances, but I'm sure there's plenty of things ADDA doesn't know about."

Wes didn't hesitate to nod. Ashley wouldn't betray them. "I sometimes talk with the leaders of StoneRiver and SkyTree. Unfortunately, StrongFalls keeps to themselves."

"Then you talk with their leaders, and I'm going to talk with your mother again to see if she can give me more details. That way, I'll have a better idea of what we should be looking for in the dense text of the ADDA handbooks and rules."

Despite the enormity of what they needed to do, Wes traced Ashley's cheek and murmured, "You're so damn amazing. With you at my side, PineRock is going to become stronger than ever."

Her cheeks colored, and he wished he could kiss her cheek, over to her mouth, and tell her with action how he admired her.

But all he could do without risking everything was bring her hand to his mouth, kiss the back of it, drop it, and say, "Then let's get to work."

Chapter Ten

Ashley finished her rather long-winded conversation with Wes's mother and retreated to the bedroom she was currently using as her base on PineRock.

Even though Cynthia had tried to casually drop questions about Wes into the conversation, Ashley had managed to keep it on track.

For the most part.

When Cynthia had dangled a story about Wes escaping the house at age two and how he'd run around the clan in his underwear until someone could catch him, she hadn't been able to pass it up.

It seemed the restrained façade Wes had used all these years hid quite a lot. Yes, he'd been a kid in the story, but she wondered if the adventurous, more carefree version of him was buried deep inside somewhere. The teasing at breakfast must've only been the start of it.

Not that finding out there was more to learn about Wes had changed her path. She wanted to mate the man and spend her life finding out everything she could about him.

However, none of that could happen if they didn't make it so she could stay on PineRock.

But thanks to Cynthia's listing of various rumors she'd heard, Ashley might just have the lead she'd been hoping for.

She quickly booted up her laptop and tapped her fingers against each other as she waited for it to load. Why had she shut it down completely? Each second that ticked by prevented her from securing her future.

Because as smart as she was, not even Ashley had memorized the ADDA handbook, rule book, or every law related to dragon-shifters in America.

When it came up, she went to the necessary folder and double-clicked on her PDF copy of the handbook used by every ADDA employee in the US. Scanning the table of contents, she found what she was looking for —*Reward Systems.*

For the most part, ADDA rarely used the reward system for dragon clans anymore. It was deemed expensive by the government, but also humiliating by the dragon clans since it treated them like children.

However, the system hadn't officially been removed from the books. And as she scanned the words, she found what she needed and read the passage:

When a clan leader has ruled over a dragon clan peacefully for at least three years and has no more than two minor violations, they can request a special license to marry a human. It is in the best interest of ADDA to foster good relations with the dragon leaders, and there's no better way to keep a close eye on a clan than to have its leader take a human spouse, especially if that spouse is an ADDA employee. If a leader decides to take up this offer, he will be subject to stricter follow-up visits and can't deny future access to ADDA employees unless he wishes to lose his human wife.

Ashley rolled her eyes at the assumption the clan leader would be a straight male. She felt sorry if a female dragon-shifter ever tried to use the loophole, let alone if a male wanted another male.

However, in her case, it didn't matter since Wes indeed wanted a wife, so she kept reading:

All that is required is a letter from the prospective wife, assuring ADDA she is becoming the dragon leader's spouse voluntarily. This will grant temporary residency on said dragon clan until the matter can be further investigated. (It is unwise to try to take away the prospective bride, as was learned in the case of Clan MountainMist in 1878.) Refer to Section Three for how to handle a clan leader bride request in greater detail. Section Four includes additional steps if the woman in question works for ADDA and wishes to continue her employment with the department.

She sat back in her chair. Since she'd been working with PineRock for years, she knew Wes met the qualifications. Well, technically. When Ryan Ford had been dropped from the sky by a dragon, the incident could've resulted in Wes's removal if it had been reported to ADDA.

However, Ryan had refused to report the incident. And for some reason, Ashley had let it slide.

Maybe because deep down, she'd held on to hope about snagging Wes for herself. And even without knowing the rule book cover to cover, she knew enough to guess that a dragon clan needed good behavior to ask for any sort of favor from ADDA.

Regardless, she now had to set things in motion. Picking up her cell phone, she sent a quick text to Wes, asking him to meet her.

When he replied he'd be there in a few minutes, Ashley scanned the additional information about how to proceed with her letter.

While her heart thumped hard at the information, she couldn't help but worry a little. If something was bound to go wrong for a dragon clan, it tended to happen. The two most recent lotteries and the ensuing unrest on PineRock had shown her that.

And Ashley didn't want to think that just as she'd found a way to be with her man, she still couldn't have him.

So instead, she focused on writing a quick draft. That way, she could at least have the first step ready to go if Wes gave her idea the green light.

WES DASHED down the stairs of the main security building, eager to hear what Ashley had found. However, before he could reach the exit, Andre Carter stepped into his path, and he said, "I need to talk with you, Wes."

Since the Protector was one of his most trusted, Wes didn't hesitate to turn around. He said, "In my office," and headed back up the stairs.

His dragon sighed. *At this rate, we'll never find out how to claim Ashley as our mate.*

This is the life of a clan leader, dragon. Would you have me ignore the clan for one female?

I wish I could say yes, but of course I won't. This is our home. And dragons protect their homes and family. Just make sure Ashley becomes part of that family soon.

How about I promise to let you shift and show your form to her when we have the chance? Will that help?

His beast grunted. *It's not as good as sex, but I'll take what I can get.*

His dragon somewhat mollified, Wes typed in the code for his office door and walked inside, Andre right on his heels. The door clicked closed just as Wes leaned against his desk. He asked the younger dragonman, "What happened?"

Andre stood taller, which usually meant the male had bad news. He cleared his throat and answered, "The ADDA police will be here in twenty or thirty minutes."

Careful not to show surprise, Wes asked calmly, "Did they say why?"

"Something about a call they received, saying a human female is being held on PineRock against her will."

He had a feeling the League bastards had called in about Ashley. "Seeing as Tori is established here and Ashley is here on ADDA business, work with the police when they get here and show them everything is as it should be."

Andre nodded and added, "They want to talk to you as well. Something about a human saying you threatened him last night?"

The fucking assholes were out to get him, too, it seemed.

No matter. Wes had dealt with false reports to the ADDA police before, and this was no different. "Then I'll work with them as well. But until they get here, I need to talk with Ashley. Can you get her from my mother's house and bring her here as quickly as possible?"

Loyal male he was, Andre bobbed his head. "Is there anything else you need me to do after that?"

"Just have some of the other Protectors keep an eye on the humans for me while the police are here. If one of the police wants to ask Tori or Ryan questions, I don't want to risk Jose or Gaby being territorial and threatening a cop. Having a Protector there will help to soothe their inner dragons and keep heads level."

His dragon growled. *It's unfair that we have to take it and can't protect our own.*

I'm not saying we can't protect our loved ones. However, I don't want to throw fuel on the fire, so to speak.

One day, we'll have greater freedom to do what we want.

Perhaps. But today isn't that day.

Wes dismissed Andre and went back to his desk. He needed to ready any and all paperwork for inspection. And the monotonous task distracted him from what Ashley had discovered.

Because if things didn't go well with the ADDA police, he might lose her anyway, even if she'd found a loophole for them to pounce upon.

Chapter Eleven

W es figured there was maybe ten minutes before the police arrived at PineRock's front gate when Ashley finally rang his doorbell. He didn't waste time answering it and quickly tugged her inside. And while he couldn't kiss her hello, he brought her against his body and held her close.

Even though her slightly dilated pupils told him she was affected as much as him—Wes didn't care if his female could feel his hardening cock—she got right down to business. "Andre didn't tell me much about why I'm here. Why do we have to talk in your office instead of your mother's house?"

He explained about the ADDA police and potential charges before adding, "So tell me quickly what you found, love. That way it won't be on my mind when I face the humans."

She searched his gaze. "Just know I'm going to help

you with them, Wes. And don't even think about telling me not to."

The corner of his mouth kicked up. "I wouldn't dare try."

She smiled and her muscles relaxed a fraction. "I found a way for us to be together *and* for me not to be kicked out of ADDA. Well, I think so."

His heart skipped a beat. "Start talking."

"Have you heard about the dragon reward system?"

He grunted. "Only vaguely, but it's been a long time since I've heard it mentioned. Why?"

As she explained about the clause concerning clan leaders and human wives, Wes did his best not to get his hopes up. Oh, he wanted Ashley Swift as his mate more than anything. But sometimes what seemed easy with ADDA turned out to be a fucking disaster in reality.

When Ashley finished the explanation, she said, "I already typed out a quick draft of the necessary letter. And while I'd like to have a little more time to make it perfect, I can access my online copy, print it out here, and have it ready for the ADDA police, just in case."

He raised his brows, unable to pass up the chance to rile her a little. "You're not even going to formally ask me to become your mate, let alone get down on one knee?"

She rolled her eyes. "Is the pomp and circumstance more important than actually being mates?"

He should drop the teasing and just scream yes. But Wes couldn't help but caress her cheek and whisper, "I've seen you on your knees before, and I rather like it."

"Wes Dalton, if you think I'm about to give you a blowjob just as the police come knocking, I'm going to reconsider being your mate."

He chuckled. "Hey, I couldn't resist. As your soon-to-be mate, it's my job to tease you at every opportunity. I think it's a little better than me trying to irritate you on purpose, right?"

"I'm not sure teasing is that much different than irritating me," she muttered.

Taking her face in his hands, he said seriously, "I love you, Ashley Swift. I have for years but resisted admitting it. So will you be my mate? I'll even go down on one knee and offer a paper ring if that's what it takes."

Her face softened. "Oh, Wes."

"Is that a yes or no?"

"Of course I'll be your damn mate. And in case you're wondering, I love you, too, you impossible dragonman."

Both man and beast mentally roared at her admission.

Ashley was going to be their mate. Not only that, but she loved them.

His dragon said, *I dare the police to try and take her away now.*

Ignoring his beast, he kissed Ashley's cheek before saying, "I will treat you like a queen and worship every inch of your body later. But for now, I think we'll celebrate by printing out that stupid letter."

She snorted. "It's probably the most original engagement story ever. A proposal celebrated with paperwork."

He nipped her jaw, loving how her breath hitched. "I don't want ordinary, let alone boring, which is why I want a life with you."

ASHLEY TRIED to think of a witty reply, but her knees were jelly, and she was having a hard time merely standing up.

Wes loved her. The strong, teasing, sometimes irritating sexy man loved her and was going to be her mate.

But despite all that, she couldn't even kiss him on the lips.

Which meant she was going to have to charm the ADDA police—something she'd done many times before—and get everything cleared up so she could officially mate Wes and start her new life.

She traced his jaw and replied, "Good, because I don't think I could do boring if I tried. Even if things turn peaceful, I'm always out to learn something new."

His pupils flashed before he said, "My dragon wants to take you up into the air at the first opportunity. That should be new for you."

Even though it was technically illegal for a dragon-shifter to take a human up into the air—barring some extreme circumstance like saving humans from a natural disaster or as part of a coordinated rescue effort—her heart rate kicked up. "I've always wanted to try it. But it'll mean lots of safety harnesses, even with those baskets some dragons use in other parts of the world."

He raised his brows. "For someone who's supposed to make sure dragons *don't* take humans flying, you sure know a lot about it."

She tilted her head. "Knowing as much as possible about dragon-shifters is my job. That means the good, the bad, and even the ugly."

A door chime interrupted any sort of reply. And even though Ashley knew this would be her life going forward —one full of constant interruptions—she hoped that one day they could have an entire conversation in one go. Maybe she'd have to see if PineRock's head Protector would help Wes out with downtime and vice versa.

Wes kissed her cheek one last time before motioning her to move behind him. Since she wasn't mated to him yet, let alone knew what all of PineRock's clan members thought of her, she followed his order.

He opened the door revealing the brown-skinned, black-haired Protector named Andre. The other dragonman said, "They're here and wanting to talk with both of you."

Wes nodded. "We'll be there in a few minutes. I just need to print out one last thing for the meeting."

Once Andre went back down the hallway, he tugged Ashley over to his computer. "Print out your letter, love. We might need it."

She did as told and took a few deep breaths to wash

away any nervousness. Oh, she had plenty of experience with the ADDA police, but a lot more was at stake this time. And Ashley was determined to be as charming, witty, and convincing as she'd ever been in her life.

So as she picked up her letter, she nodded at Wes. "Let's go and sort out the beginning of the rest of our lives."

He took her hand a brief second before releasing it. However, the flitting contact calmed her further.

Ashley and her dragonman would make this all work out.

They had to.

Chapter Twelve

W es did his best to push away his concerns about Ashley. She could handle herself, and he knew it, but it was still hard for a dragonman to completely ignore his instinct to protect what was his.

His beast growled. *Don't worry, we'll do whatever it takes to keep her here with us.*

Not wanting to waste energy on arguing about Ashley allowing anyone to "keep" her, he ignored his dragon and entered the main conference room.

He sat down across from three human men, ranging in age from thirty to probably mid-fifties, all wearing the gray uniforms of the ADDA police. Their golden dragon-shaped badged gleamed a little under the light.

Ashley slid into the chair next to him, which wouldn't be unusual even if she wasn't about to become his mate. After all, she was, for all purposes, his representative to the human world. No one would be able to tell that he could hear each breath of hers, or how her heart raced a little faster than normal.

Under the eagle-eyed brown gaze of the deputy police chief for the area, he didn't dare risk taking her hand under the table, either. Since he'd met Officer Garcia before, Wes nodded in greeting. "Hello, Officer Garcia."

The human male in his fifties with black hair peppered with gray returned the greeting. "I'm a little surprised to be here, Dalton. Of all the clan leaders in the area, you're usually the most well-behaved."

He resisted clenching his jaw at the remark. Garcia was doing his job and didn't think anything about how his words made Wes and the other leaders sound like children.

Keeping his voice neutral, Wes asked, "So what can I help you with, officer?"

Garcia's eyes darted to Ashley and back. "Were you out with Ms. Swift in Reno last night? Specifically at a bar called *Deuces Wild*?"

There was no reason to lie. "Yes. I participated in the orphan charity auction, and Ms. Swift had the winning bid. ADDA can give you all the details and confirm I was there."

"Your participation was already confirmed. It's what happened after Ms. Swift won you that worries me." Garcia flipped open the folder on the table in front of him and read, "The tall, auburn-haired dragonman threatened me with growls, flashing eyes, and I saw him clench his fingers into fists. If I hadn't left, he would've attacked me. Even if he didn't threaten with words, it was intimidation. He's not supposed to do that in human places, and I feared for my life."

Wes suppressed another growl that threatened to emerge and waited for Garcia to ask him a question. After all, the less he said to the police, the better. That way words couldn't be twisted later on if he was actually charged.

However, Garcia looked at Ashley when he spoke again. "The person who made the complaint is the brother-in-law of Duncan Parrish. Parrish said you were being taken against your will. Is this true?"

If it had been just him and Ashley, he knew that her temper would've flared. However, her cool, collected ADDA persona was fully in place as she replied, "Of course not, Carlos. I won Dalton in the charity auction and wanted to see him lose at darts." She shrugged a shoulder. "It's not every day you can trounce a dragon-shifter, let alone a clan leader."

Garcia spoke again. "So it was just darts and nothing else? Parrish suggested there was more between you, mainly on Dalton's side. He was worried he might try to kidnap you and force you to be his mate."

His dragon growled inside his head. Wes had known little about Parrish before the meeting at the bar, but the male was definitely on his shit list now.

Ashley replied, "Yes, it was only to play darts at first. As for my feelings about Mr. Dalton, they shouldn't be

Mr. Parrish's business. However, now that you mention it, let me show you that any relationship between us is covered legally." She pushed her letter toward the officer. "Per the ADDA rule book, Dalton qualifies to take a human female as his wife. This is my letter of intent to marry, and the ceremony will be held as soon as ADDA gives the green light."

Garcia blinked and scanned the letter. Once done, he met Ashley's eyes again. "Are you sure about this, Ms. Swift? If he's forcing you, just say something, and I'll escort you off PineRock straight away."

Anger churned inside Wes's stomach. He wanted to shout at the bastard and tell him off. However, restraint was the only way he was going to win this round. So he let Ashley answer for him. "No one is being forced, Carlos." She leaned forward and smiled. "Do you think anyone could really force me to do something?" She gestured toward the youngest male in the room. "Johnson there knows firsthand about that."

Johnson's cheeks turned pink, and he cleared his throat. However, it was Garcia who spoke. "And how Johnson treated you was why he was demoted." He paused and then said, "Are you sure about this, Ashley? You're one of the most competent ADDA liaisons I've worked with over the last twenty years. I'd hate to lose you."

She beamed at Garcia, and it took every ounce of strength Wes had not to haul her against his side and glare at the other males. His human said, "Oh, that won't be changing." She tapped the letter. "This is the protocol for marrying a dragon-shifter. However, because Dalton qualifies under the reward system, it means I should still be able to work with ADDA, too." She winked. "I'll be keeping you and your guys in line for a while yet, Carlos."

Garcia barked a laugh. "Good. Otherwise, I might have more paperwork than I already do."

His dragon murmured, *Our female is charming and very, very good at managing them.*

I suppose, he muttered.

Ashley motioned toward her letter. "That should clear everything up about me being here by choice. As for the complaint lodged against Wes that says he threatened the human, Wes was merely trying to help me. One of the human guys wanted me to leave without Dalton, no matter my own desires. If Wes hadn't stepped up, along with the bar's security guard, I'm not sure what would've happened. I want to say the other guy might've tried to force me to leave or might even have tried to hurt Wes just to scare me."

Garcia frowned. "Do you want to press charges? If he hurt you, I'll risk Duncan Parrish's wrath."

Wes nearly blinked. It seemed Ashley did indeed have a very good relationship with the ADDA police. That could most definitely be a blessing in disguise later on, once she was officially his mate.

Ashley waved a hand in dismissal. "No, it's fine. As long as the other side's charge is dismissed, I won't bother. I'd much rather focus on my upcoming marriage and move to PineRock."

Garcia's eye finally met his again. "You'd better treat her right, Dalton. If not, then I don't care if I get fired, I'll kick your ass into next week."

His dragon snorted but thankfully didn't say anything so Wes could reply, "I will treasure her every day, sir. And if anyone threatens her, then consequences be damned, I'll do what it takes to protect her."

For the first time in their acquaintance, Wes swore respect flashed in Garcia's eyes. "I like that answer." He reached into his pocket, took out a card, and held it out. "This is my private number. If something goes wrong and Ashley is in danger, call me. I'll help how I can."

Doing his best not to let his surprise show, Wes took the card and nodded. "Thank you."

Ashley clapped her hands. "Are you two done discussing me as if I'm some sort of wilting flower that will be crushed in a light breeze?"

Garcia stood. "Yes, we're done. I'll make sure the charges are dropped. But maybe the pair of you could stay on PineRock for a while and not go into the city? Just to give everyone some space and a chance for cooler heads later on."

Wes stood. "My mate will keep me busy. Although there have been some humans trespassing around the edges of our land lately. So I may need to call you sooner than I'd like to protect Ashley."

With one last bob of his head, Garcia exited the room, and his two other officers followed suit.

As soon as they were alone, Wes hauled Ashley up against his front and cupped her cheek. "Do you know how hard it was for me to let you flirt with them and not do anything?"

"There's a difference between flirting and being charming, Wes. I used the latter on them. From now on, I'll only use the former on you. Mostly."

"Mostly?" He growled.

She smiled. "Well, I don't want to throw away something I could use to better fit in here. Sometimes flirting with older men can be helpful, even when we both know it's harmless."

His dragon snorted. *Let her charm the grandpas. That will only help the humans on PineRock anyway since most of the older generation are still a little biased.*

Wes replied to his female, stroking her cheek as he said, "As much as I like your long-term strategies, I think we need to address our mating first." His eyes darted to her lips. "And making sure we can have our frenzy sooner rather than later." Ashley licked her lips, and Wes groaned. "You did that on purpose."

She moved a finger to where his neckline met his skin and gently rubbed back and forth, each pass making his cock harder. "No, I didn't. There's just something about you that turns me into all those things I thought were clichés—weak knees, racing heart, and throbbing lips." She leaned a fraction closer. "So I'm definitely on board for making our mating official and having our frenzy. I'm rather looking forward to the frenzy. After all, I've heard so much about it over the years. It'll be nice to have some firsthand experience."

He moved his hand from her cheek to thread it through her hair and tug her even closer until he could feel the heat of her breath on his skin. "Good, then it means I won't have to hold back or try not to scare you."

"You could never scare me, Wes. I love you and trust you to the moon and back."

"Despite your ever-growing list of clichés, I love you, too. And I'll always hold your trust close to my heart."

His dragon grunted. *Stop with the pretty words. Kiss her cheek, her neck, even her hand, but something.*

Not wanting to argue, he leaned over and took her earlobe between his teeth. After biting lightly, he moved to kiss down her neck until Ashley dug her nails into his back. Her breathless words might've been lost to a human, but Wes heard every word as she murmured, "I wish you could be inside me right now."

He replied, "Soon, love. Soon I'll be inside you, around you, kissing you everywhere, and then some." Wes leaned back and took her chin in his hand to lift her face toward his. "Although if you want me to strip you and tease you between those pretty thighs, just say the word."

Ashley groaned. "No. Because I have a feeling if I'm naked with you again, I'll want much more than that. It's best not to tempt either one of us."

He kissed her nose. "Then let's file the paperwork and get things in motion so that the next time you're naked with me, we won't have to stop."

She nodded before gently pushing against his chest. With herculean effort, Wes stepped back and moved to the door.

As they made their way to his office, Wes did his best to cool his libido and soften his dick. Because he needed as much blood to his brain as he could manage to make things happen quickly. He was impatient to claim his female completely.

Chapter Thirteen

The next three days flew by as Ashley filed some paperwork, talked with her ADDA superiors, and arranged for her things to be packed and moved from her apartment—Wes hadn't trusted her going alone, and she'd finally capitulated.

But as she looked in the mirror and straightened the dress Wes's mother had gifted for her mating ceremony, Ashley couldn't help but smile. The dark blue dress made her eyes pop, and she loved how it fitted tight around her chest and flared out, almost like some sort of fairy-tale dress.

Which meant she couldn't resist swirling one way and then the other, just because.

Although comparing her dress to a fairy tale wasn't that far off. After all, she was about to marry a mythical creature—a dragon-shifter—and move to his realm—his clan—for her happily ever after.

Not only had ADDA approved her application to mate, they'd also created a new post for her called "Pine-Rock liaison officer." She would have her man and the career she loved so much. It looked like all her dreams were going to come true after all.

Well, for the most part.

Sure, there were enemies still out there, and no doubt the day would come when Duncan Parrish and the League would most likely target her and cause even more trouble. But for the here and now, things were perfect. And Ashley was determined to enjoy the present while she could.

A knock on the door garnered her attention, and she said, "Come in."

Cynthia entered and walked over to her with a smile on her face. "I have a feeling my son is going to do a lot of growling tonight. Lots of males are going to notice you."

A clan leader's mating ceremony was a little more involved, Ashley had learned. They'd have to stick around for a few hours to celebrate with the clan, unlike most mated pairs who could sneak off and start their honeymoons straight after the ceremony.

Ashley shrugged. "It's not like I haven't heard him growl a million times before. Although he'd better be prepared for me to do the same, if any other woman tries to flirt with him tonight."

The dragonwoman snorted. "I still think you were a dragon-shifter in another life."

As they smiled at one another, a sense of peace came over Ashley. Cynthia had been nothing but supportive but also respected boundaries. No mother-in-law from hell for Ashley. "We'll never know. Although my children will be half dragon-shifter, which means a lot of cramming before any of them arrive."

ADDA books didn't exactly cover the child-rearing practices of dragon-shifters.

Cynthia laughed. "Don't worry, the entire clan will want to help." She lowered her voice. "But my advice is to set boundaries early, or you'll have twenty people all trying to raise the little one with different rules."

Before she could reply, there was another knock followed by Cris entering the room. Ashley blinked. She'd never seen the head Protector wear a dress before.

Cris rolled her eyes. "I can be tough and still be feminine on occasion."

"Of course," she murmured. "You look nice."

Cris glanced down at her bright green dress. "I figure the super bright color will make me visible, and people will know I'm watching them."

"And there's the head of security part of you coming out," Ashley pointed out.

Cris shrugged. "It's who I am. And even when I try to turn off for a while, it just doesn't work."

Ashley wished she was a little closer to the head Protector. Someday she wanted to talk with the dragonwoman about taking some time for herself. Between what she'd seen and what Wes had mentioned, Cris worked harder than anyone else on PineRock, even Wes.

But as music drifted in from the large room down the hall, Ashley added it to her ever-growing list of shit to do. Yes, she'd help Cris, just not today. Until Ashley was officially mated to Wes, her future wasn't entirely secure.

This day, and the ensuing frenzy, were for her. After that, she'd start crafting plans for her new home.

One of the Protectors appeared in the doorway to collect Ashley. She murmured her goodbyes and tried her best to ignore her pounding heart. Not out of fear or nervousness, but excitement. The future she'd only ever dreamed about was coming true in a matter of minutes.

WES STOOD at one side of the raised platform and tried to distract himself by watching the clan gathered below.

It'd been a while since they'd had any sort of big celebration. Not because the clan didn't like such events, but he'd been too busy rooting out and transferring the clan members who had tried to hurt the two humans, Tori and Ryan.

And not for the first time, Wes felt a little guilty at his neglect of the clan as a whole.

His dragon spoke up. *It was better to make the clan a safe space again. Now we can have those kinds of parties and not worry about someone targeting the humans.*

Wes noticed Gaby trying her best to dance with her human male, but failing badly at it. He smiled and replied, *I know. But it's hard not to compare myself to former leaders and how they ran things.*

We're different for many reasons. It's been decades since a Pine-Rock leader has mated a human.

It was true. And to be honest, Wes had thought it impossible.

Then he spotted Ashley at the other side of the stage, and his mind promptly forgot about everything but his beautiful human.

Her blue dress made her eyes and skin glow. And the soft waves of her normally straight hair made her appear more innocent. Then he met her gaze, saw the humor dancing there, and knew that even if she changed appearances for a special event, it was still the female he loved inside.

Hell, she could wear a trash bag and he'd still think her fucking beautiful.

His dragon chimed in. *What she wears doesn't matter because we're going to be tearing it off soon.*

Before he could reprimand his beast about not destroying Ashley's mating dress, Cris appeared behind him and whispered, "Come on, Wes. It's time to get this done."

He never took his gaze from Ashley as he replied, "Who knew you could be such a romantic?"

"Whatever, dumbass. Do you want to mate her or not? Because I'm the one who has to do it."

Usually the clan leader led the ceremony, but in his case, the head Protector would take his place. He whispered, "Of course I do. But I have to admit I can't wait for the day when it's your turn. I'm going to tease you relentlessly."

Cris grunted. "Let's just get this started."

Wes had a feeling there was someone Cris liked, but she could be extremely closed off when it came to her personal wants.

But he added it to his list of things to investigate. Because his head Protector deserved someone who made her feel as happy as Ashley did him.

Taking a deep breath, he took the first step toward the center of the platform, and then another, until he and Ashley met in the middle. A tall stand with a carved box sat right behind them, which was where Cris stood. The clan quieted down in anticipation.

Reaching out a hand, he took Ashley's and squeezed it. She smiled at him, love and happiness in her eyes, and he almost pinched himself to make sure he wasn't dreaming.

His dragon growled. *If you don't stop with all these flowery words, I'm going to wrestle control away from you and hurry this the hell up.*

Since he knew his dragon would never ruin their mating ceremony—the dragon half didn't care about traditions, but understood the importance—Wes brushed off the words and memorized Ashley's blue eyes, pale cheeks, and dark hair.

Finally Cris spoke loudly, her voice carrying throughout the large room. "Today is a happy day for Clan PineRock. Our leader has not only found his mate, but they also discovered how to be together despite the odds stacked against them." She picked up the box and continued, "Inside are the gifts we give to every newly mated pair, including a set of rings engraved with a unique message written in the old dragon language." She opened it, plucked out the two rings, and offered them to Wes. "May your mating be happy, full of laughter, and fruitful."

He heard a faint snort from Ashley and resisted laughing. Even though the last sentence was traditional, he couldn't imagine his human liking the fruitful part. Not because she didn't want children—she said she did—but at the word choice.

His beast growled to remind him to focus. So Wes took the rings with one hand and began his necessary speech. "For far too long, I tried to deny and push aside what I felt for you. I thought finding a way for a clan leader and an ADDA employee to be together was too difficult, too impossible, too 'insert an excuse here.' It took you bidding on me and forcing me to drop my clan leader exterior I used as a shield against your charm, wits, and beauty for me to realize how I've been a fool all this time. I love your fire, your huge heart, and the fact you know how to push my buttons better than anyone. I love you, Ashley Swift." He held up the smaller of the two rings. "With this band, I stake my claim on you. Do you accept?"

She extended her ring finger. "I do."

Once the gold was in place, a small thrill coursed through his body at the sight.

However, he couldn't take more than a moment to memorize the feeling because Ashley took the other band and said, "For the longest time, I thought I had to choose between my job and the guy I wanted more than any other. I stuck to the rules, believing there was no way to have both. And yet, for one night, I decided to skirt the edge of the rules and spend some time with a smart, intelligent, sexy guy who could be as stubborn as me. Maybe the night didn't go quite as planned, but it was exactly what we both needed. We are better together in so many ways, and going forward, we'll be happy and all that, yes. But we'll also make sure PineRock is safe and secure for our children and beyond. I love you, Wes Dalton, more than anything." She held up the ring in her hand. "With this band, I stake my claim on you. Do you accept?"

Since she held the ring between her fingers, he moved his own so he could put it through the top. She laughed as she moved it the rest of the way down.

Cris spoke up again, per the custom. "Then, as Pine-Rock's head Protector, I proclaim you two mates, bound by both human and dragon law and under PineRock's eternal protection. You may kiss your mate."

For once not caring about what the clan thought of him, Wes pulled Ashley against his body, cupped her cheek, and murmured, "This is just a promise for later."

Not wanting to start a mate-claim frenzy, he kissed her cheek, her jaw, and even her nose before placing one final kiss on her forehead. For a few beats, they merely held each other, almost as if they were making the ceremony final by being as close as possible while still clothed.

Then the applause erupted from the clan, yanking him back to reality. Taking Ashley's hand, he kissed the back of it before facing the crowd and asking, "Who's ready to meet my new mate?"

As the clan situated themselves around the edges of the room to form the greeting lines, he hauled Ashley against his side and whispered, "Do I need to prepare myself for some grandpa flirting?"

She snorted. "Maybe." She moved her head to his ear and spoke softly so that the others couldn't hear her. "But for every grandpa or grandma I flirt with, I'll make it up to you when we're alone."

Blood rushed south, and it took everything he had to keep his dick in line. He murmured back into her ear, "Then I hope you flirt with each and every one of them."

Laughing, Ashley shook her head. "My, my, how your tune has changed."

Before he could tease her back, they reached the first family in the line. Wes managed to pack away his urge to tease, flirt, and fuck his mate so he could perform his official duties.

Because the faster he did them, the sooner he would finally be able to kiss Ashley on the mouth and claim her with his cock.

And that couldn't come fast enough.

Chapter Fourteen

Ashley lost track of time as she smiled, chatted, and tried being friendly with as many of her new clan members as she could. Not everyone was open and welcoming, but none were outright hostile, either.

And considering she'd been the representative of an agency that restricted so many aspects of their lives, she couldn't blame them.

The interactions only strengthened her resolve to make even greater changes in not only ADDA-dragon relations but to lobby for more freedoms, too. After all, from everything she'd read, it seemed to be working in the UK. Maybe it was finally the US's time to shine.

However, as she said her goodbyes to the final family in the greeting line, Cris's voice boomed over the loudspeaker, ending any further thoughts on reform. "Okay, I think it's more than time for Wes and his new mate to leave and have their own kind of celebration.

If you missed your chance to give a welcome greeting, you can do it later, after they've finished with the frenzy."

Even though the dragon-shifters around her merely smiled and gave knowing looks, Ashley's cheeks burned.

She wasn't exactly used to everyone knowing she was about to have sex many times over.

Wes's comforting whisper filled her ear. "One more thing ADDA doesn't teach you about my kind—dragons aren't embarrassed by sex. So get used to it, because once the frenzy is over, everyone will tease you."

"Great," she muttered.

He chuckled and hugged her closer to his side. "It's not like we have live video feeds or anything." He lowered his voice for her ears only. "What happens in the bedroom is only between us. And trust me, I have a lot of things to show you there that could make you blush. So get some of your blushing out of the way now."

She lightly hit his chest and willed her face not to turn any redder. "Can we leave yet?"

Wes gave one more wave to the room and then scooped Ashley into his arms. He projected his voice. "Cris and Troy are in charge until I emerge again. Try not to wreak havoc while I'm busy enjoying my new mate."

And even if she couldn't see them, she could feel her cheeks burn hotter. She hoped the dragon-shifters weren't so comfortable that they traded sex stories in clan gatherings, for all to hear. Because if so, Ashley was going to have to get over some of her embarrassment as soon as possible.

Maybe she could even rope Wes into it, making it a sort of game.

Wes walked quickly out of the room. They were soon alone as he carried her into the night, the cool air helping to tame her burning cheeks. And as she snuggled into his chest, the remaining irritation and embarrassment faded away. Instead, she was intensely aware of his hard, hot chest at her side, as well as the uniquely masculine scent that was Wes.

Even though she was only a little cold in the night air, her nipples tightened in anticipation of what was coming.

After all this time, she was finally going to claim Wes and have him claim her in return. She blurted a question she'd been dying to ask but hadn't found the courage to do so until now. "Will your dragon come out at first?"

Wes shook his head. "No, I'll be claiming you the first time. But he'll come out after that." He met her eyes in the fading light. "Are you afraid of him? I would've liked more time to let you get to know him, but it didn't really work out that way."

His concern only made her love him more. "Don't worry, I'm not so much afraid as I am curious. After all, you hear lots of rumors and occasionally gossip from the humans mated to dragon-shifters. And it's almost entirely positive."

Wes's pupils flashed to slits and back. "He says it

should be all positive. But really, my dragon is just a little upset he couldn't show his magnificent dragon form to you before claiming you."

She smiled up at him. "Then tell him to make this frenzy count and set some kind of record. The sooner we finish, the sooner we can do other things."

Wes laughed. "I know you like to be efficient, but I don't think that'll work in this case." His voice dropped an octave. "Nor do I want to rush claiming my female."

His words made her shiver and wetness rush between her thighs. Maybe having a long frenzy wouldn't be a bad thing. Sure, she'd get sore. But her heart raced at the thought of a strong, dominant dragonman claiming her over and over again.

Wes groaned. "You're killing me, Ash. I can tell you want me, but I'm not about to claim you in the middle of the clan, where anyone could see."

She tilted her head. "Maybe eventually we can try a remote location sometime. I've always wanted to have sex outside."

He groaned again, and she laughed. He said, "You are going to be the death of me, human. I can just feel it."

"If by death you mean your perfect match in every way, then yes, that's me."

Eyes heated, Wes said firmly, "I already know you're my perfect match, and not just because fate said so." He repositioned her in his arms to hold her tighter against his chest. "Now, hold on because I'm going to run so I can show you."

As she looped her arms around his neck and laid her head on his chest, she reveled in his breathing, his heartbeat, and even the slight breeze on her skin.

There was a time for teasing and talking and a time for other things. This was one of the latter.

So Ashley remained silent to let Wes run as fast as possible to their new home. Because she might just be more eager than him to ditch her clothes and ride him like there was no tomorrow.

WES TRIED to restrain himself as he ran to his house, but the pounding need of both man and dragon to claim their mate ran strong.

He was starting to understand why most new mates raced from their ceremony minutes after finishing instead of lingering around. It was almost as if making a clan leader wait several hours was a new test of its own. One that was almost as trying as when he'd gone through his leadership competition.

His dragon spoke up. *That part is over, so stop thinking about it. Just make sure not to waste time once we're inside our house. You have the rest of our lives to talk with our mate. The frenzy is more important.*

For once, Wes didn't argue with his beast.

He finally reached his house, managed to open the

door—he'd left it unlocked on purpose—and went inside, shutting the door with his foot in the process.

Since he wanted to claim his mate in their bedroom, he ran the short distance and then gently laid Ashley on his—no, their—bed.

As she leaned on her elbows and stared up at him with her dark blue eyes, his already hard cock turned to granite. He growled, "Either take off that dress or I'm ripping it off."

Not waiting for an answer since he knew Ashley was as aroused as him, Wes concentrated on shucking his own clothes. Once the tattered remains lay on the floor, he moved even closer to the bed.

Satisfaction coursed through him as Ashley pushed the dress down her legs and tossed it to the floor. She laid back, her arms over her head as she met his gaze again and stated, "I'm waiting."

No hesitation, no fear, nothing negative. His mate was willing to accept all of him.

He slowly crawled above her on his hands and knees until his face was right over hers. Then he lay on her, sucking in a breath as her warm skin met his.

Ignoring his dragon's roars to fuck her already, he cupped her cheek and moved until his lips were an inch away from hers. "This is the only time I'm going to take it slow, Ash. A dragon in a frenzy is demanding, insatiable, and driven by the need to fuck you until you're pregnant. Are you ready?"

She lifted her hips, pressing against his cock, and he

groaned. Her voice was husky as she said, "I've been ready for years. Kiss me, Wes. And show me what you got."

Maybe he should take his time, lingering and savoring their first kiss. But between his dragon's need, the feel of his mate's skin against his, and the scent of her arousal, he came down hard on her lips, pushing his tongue into her mouth, and claiming her in rough strokes.

The need to fuck her coursed through his body, his dragon all but throwing a tantrum as he said, *Hurry, hurry. You get the first time only because you promised not to hesitate. So start, or I'll claim it.*

Since there was no way in hell he was going to let that happen, Wes continued to kiss her as he raised his lower body a little. Taking his cock in one hand, he ran it through Ashley's folds. He broke the kiss as he groaned. "You're so fucking wet already."

She managed to spread her legs wider. "Then don't keep me waiting."

With a shout, he pushed his cock into her pussy slowly. "You're so tight. I just want to thrust, but I don't want to hurt you."

"You'll never hurt me, Wes. Don't hold back who you are. I want that man in my bed. Man and dragon, actually. I love you."

Her words unleashed every instinct and need he'd been fighting against. Wes pushed inside her to the hilt, loving how tight and hot she was, as well as the way she gripped him as if she'd never let go.

Ashley's nails dug into his back, and it triggered his inner beast. Wes crushed his mouth against hers again, stroking against her tongue as he moved his hips.

The combination of her taste in his mouth and her heat around his dick nearly made him come straight away. But he held back, wanting—no, needing—for her to come before he did. It was one of the things a male should always do for his female.

So he rolled to his back, never breaking their connection, and finally released her mouth. "Ride me."

She blinked a second but began rocking her hips forward and back. As much as he wanted to watch her breasts bounce and tease her nipples, he had something more important to do if he wanted his mate to orgasm before him.

Wes moved his hand to her clit and circled around it, loving how she arched into his touch. Ashley groaned and murmured, "Touch me harder, Wes."

"Grip me like you mean it first."

When her insides clenched around his cock, Wes groaned.

Fuck, he could already tell that he'd never be bored of his mate in bed.

He'd have to test her willingness to listen to orders later.

For now, he merely clenched his abdominal muscles to hold back his orgasm as he swirled, flicked, and lightly pinched Ashley's clit. Every sound she made told him what she liked, what she craved.

His dragon roared. *Stop experimenting. Give her what she likes. I want a turn. Hurry.*

Since his dragon's control was close to shattering, he met Ashley's gaze as he pinched her tight bud, released, and repeated the process.

She never ceased moving her hips as she murmured, "So close, Wes. Kiss me as I come."

He managed to sit up and hold her close with one arm, never ceasing his attentions to her clit. He crushed his lips against hers, thrusting his tongue into her mouth, claiming it as hard as she was riding him.

She screamed into his mouth as she spasmed around his dick. Wes roared and let go, loving how she bucked even harder, his semen making her orgasm spiral higher.

When she finally slumped against him, he released her mouth and stroked her hair. He murmured, "My dragon isn't going to wait much longer, love. Can you handle him?"

"Of course. Although I may be a little boneless for a few minutes, so don't ask too much of me until my strength returns."

His beast said, *That doesn't matter. She's willing, and I want her.*

Before Wes could reply to Ashley, his dragon pushed to the forefront of his mind, taking control of his body. His beast gently picked Ashley up and tossed her on her stomach. As he lifted her hips and sought her pussy, Wes wished he could be the one claiming her again.

But his dragon was a part of him, and when it came to mates, they'd always share.

So he merely watched and waited until he could have her again.

ASHLEY HAD NEVER HAD another orgasm start while she was still riding the previous one.

It seemed that tidbit about dragon-shifters and their true mates, and how a dragonman's semen triggered ecstasy, wasn't rumor or fantasy.

However, before she could think more on it or even tease Wes about it, she was facedown on the mattress, her hips raised in the air.

Wes's slightly deeper voiced reached her ears. She knew from when he'd let his dragon out the other day that his beast was now in charge. "You're mine. Only mine. Say it."

Knowing the dragon half needed to hear it, she replied, "I'm yours."

She felt his cock at her entrance, and in the next beat, he thrust in to the hilt.

She cried out in a mixture of pleasure with a hint of pain.

However, before she could think more about it, Wes's dragon moved their hips in time to his thrusts, and she forgot about everything but how deep he reached inside her.

Wes's beast said, "You're mine. I need to fuck you until you carry my babe. Only then will others leave my mate alone."

Since she knew he wouldn't be rational right now, she merely arched her back. "Then stop talking and get to it."

He roared and thrust harder. Something hard brushed her clit, and she moved against what had to be the talon he'd extended from his nail. "Touch me, dragon. Show me how much your mate means to you."

Since dragons didn't like to back down from a challenge, he lightly tapped the hard talon against her clit, careful to keep the sharp point from stabbing her.

With each tap and thrust, alternating to drive her mad, she gripped the sheets harder.

She was going to like being a dragon-shifter's mate.

He finally roared, and an orgasm rushed through her, pleasure making her all but blind for a second, heightened by the fact Wes's beast still thrust into her and teased her clit.

When she finally came down, an arm went around her waist, and she felt a light kiss to her shoulder. Wes's normal voice filled her ear. "Are you all right, love?"

She turned her head so she could see his face and smiled. "More than all right."

He searched her gaze, concern in his eyes. "You're not afraid or mad at my dragon, are you?"

She laughed. "Far from it." She raised a hand to his cheek. "I meant it before—I love all of you, Wes Dalton. So if your dragon was holding back, he doesn't have to next time."

His pupils flashed before replying, "You may regret that later. But at least it placated him a little, meaning you can have a short rest before we go again."

She turned so she could sit on the mattress and be almost eye-level with Wes. She kissed him gently. "Just a short one. Maybe hold me and kiss me a few times? As much as I like it rough sometimes, slow and easy can be good, too."

He lay down on his side, and she faced him. Wes traced her jaw, her shoulder, and down her side until he rested a hand on her hip. "I can't guarantee that I'll always be able to control my dragon, but I'll remember it for when I'm in charge." The corner of his mouth ticked up. "Although not every time. The human male part also likes it rough sometimes."

She gave a devilish smile. "Good."

He blinked in surprise. Needing to feel his skin against hers, she snuggled closer. "Stop worrying about me. Seriously. I can handle it all. Well, provided you feed me every once in a while. Is there some sort of dragon frenzy delivery service?"

He chuckled, and she felt his muscles relax. "There is, actually. Because as much as I can give you short rests for food, the bathroom, and sometimes even a shower, there's no way my dragon will let you take time out to cook. He'll see it as a waste of time."

She kissed his lips briefly. "Hey, if I don't have to cook, I'm a happy person."

As they smiled at each other, Ashley could hardly believe it was real. She'd beaten the odds to find her happy ending with a dragon-shifter. And not just any dragon-shifter, but the sexiest, most perfect match for her.

So when he took her again, repeatedly, over the ensuing days, Ashley didn't notice her exhaustion or any other negative thing. No, all she knew was that she was spending time with the man she loved, and it was perfect.

Epilogue

Years later

Wes stood with his young son, Ben, in his arms, smiling as he watched Ashley splashing in the cold water of Lake Tahoe with some of the other females.

Even though he'd tried to warn that the water was too cold for her since she was finally pregnant with their second child, she'd merely raised her brows and given her best "watch me" look before diving in.

Although, in retrospect, it wasn't all bad watching his dripping-wet female splash around in the water.

His dragon snorted. *And you say I'm bad.*

One of the other clan leaders, David Lee from Stone-River, walked up to him and chuckled. "Our mates aren't going to put up with all of our protective bullshit. If you don't know that after how many years of being mated, then no one can help you."

He glanced over at the slightly older male. "Says the male who declared he'd never have a mate because they were a weakness."

David rolled his eyes. "How many times are you going to bring that up?"

Wes grinned as he readjusted his sleeping son against his shoulder. "As many times as I can. After all, you wouldn't have your mate if not for us."

The other leader muttered, "Maybe, maybe not."

He raised his brows. "The only reason Tiffany ever came to live near all of us is because her brother mated one of my clan members. You're always going to owe me for that, David."

Ashley screeched, and he watched from the corner of his eyes as Tiffany and Gaby both dunked her in the water.

Of course, Ashley laughed when she surfaced and went after Gaby for revenge.

His dragon spoke up. *Why can't we shift and join them in the lake? You can give our son to our mother. She'll watch him.*

Wes glanced down at the little boy passed out against his shoulder. *Not yet. The last few years have been busy, and I just want to spend time with our son.*

David interrupted his conversation. "Trust me, I'd rather be over there with my mate, too. But we need to meet with the other two leaders from SkyTree and StrongFalls before the official ceremony begins."

Ah, yes. The alliance treaty that the four clans near Lake Tahoe had managed to form with ADDA's blessing.

Drool dribbled from his son's mouth, and Wes wiped it away. "I'll meet you there. I need to find my mom and hand over Ben first."

With a nod, the StoneRiver leader walked toward the raised platform about a hundred feet away.

Wes took one more second to kiss his son's cheek before looking over at Ashley, willing her to meet his gaze.

She must've felt it because she looked up with a grin before blowing a kiss. He mouthed, "I love you," and she did the same.

After a quick nod to let her know he needed to leave, Wes held his son close and went to find his mother. The sooner he got the stupid ceremony done, the sooner he could spend more time with his beautiful mate and son.

Not that he had much space to complain about. After all, from today, his clan would be mostly protected from the League, he'd have official allies, and not to mention stronger working ties with ADDA. Still, despite all that, Ashley and his son were his greatest treasures, ones he'd never take for granted as long as he lived.

The Dragon's Charge

TAHOE DRAGON MATES #4

Brad Harper has known that the human bar owner, Natasha Jenkins, is his true mate since he first met her by chance on a night out with friends. However, after his first mate ran off with a human, he's held a grudge. He only took the job in the bar as a favor to his clan leader. But when both Natasha's bar and her life are in jeopardy, he has no choice but to protect her. The only question is if he can resist her.

Natasha Jenkins likes setting goals and achieving them. It's how she was able to set up a successful bar in Reno and be her own boss. However, when some trouble-makers show up and soon start harassing her clientele, hoping to put her out of business, she struggles with what to do. Then there's a threat to her life and she finds herself swept into the unknown world of dragon-shifters.

One dragonman in particular seems to both hate her and want to protect her at any cost.

When Natasha has no choice to but to accept a fake marriage, she soon learns more about the dragonman who used to work for her. And just when she thinks maybe she can craft a new life plan, trouble shows up again. Except this time, it could destroy everything she holds dear once and for all.

NOTE: This is a quick, steamy standalone story about fated mates and sexy dragon-shifters near Lake Tahoe in the USA. You don't have to read all my other dragon books to enjoy this one!

THE DRAGON'S CHARGE will be available in paperback in late November 2020.

The Dragon's Dilemma

LOCHGUARD HIGHLAND DRAGONS #1

In order to pay for her father's life-saving cancer treatment, Holly Anderson offers herself up as a sacrifice and sells the vial of dragon's blood. In return, she will try to bear a Scottish dragon-shifter a child. While the dragonman assigned to her is kind, Holly can't stop looking at his twin brother. It's going to take everything she has to sleep with her assigned dragonman. If she breaks the sacrifice contract and follows her heart, she'll go to jail and not be able to take care of her father.

Even though he's not ready to settle down, Fraser MacKenzie supports his twin brother's choice to take a female sacrifice to help repopulate the clan. Yet as Fraser gets to know the lass, his dragon starts demanding something he can't have—his brother's sacrifice.

Holly and Fraser fight the pull between them, but one nearly stolen kiss will change everything. Will they risk breaking the law and betraying Fraser's twin? Or, will they find a way out of the sacrifice contract and live their own happily ever after?

The Dragon's Dilemma is available in paperback.

Author's Note

I hope you enjoyed Wes and Ashley's story! I hinted at it for two books and couldn't wait to get them together. They're both fun, strong, and just plain awesome.

Originally this series was planned to be three books. However, readers really like it so while writing this one, I decided to do at least three more. For the next three we'll be focusing on another clan near Tahoe—StoneRiver. The fourth Tahoe book will be about Tasha and Brad (the bar owner and security guy from this story). After that, Ryan Ford's sister, Tiffany, will be finding her mate with the leader of StoneRiver, David Lee (which you met in the epilogue). I can't wait to get to started on them!

And now I have some people to thank for getting this out into the world:

- To Becky Johnson and her team at Hot Tree Editing. They always catch the tiniest inconsistencies and Becky just gets me by now, which makes it so much easier.
- To all my beta readers—Sabrina D., Donna H., Sandy H., and Iliana G., you do an amazing job at finding those lingering typos and minor inconsistencies.

And as always, a huge thank you to you, the reader, for either enjoying my dragons for the first time, or for following me from my longer books to this series. Writing is the best job in the world and it's your support that makes it so I can keep doing it.

Until next time, happy reading!

PS—To keep up-to-date with new releases and other goodies, please join my newsletter here.

Also by Jessie Donovan

The Dragon's Dilemma (LHD #1)

The Dragon Guardian (LHD #2)

The Dragon's Heart (LHD #3)

The Dragon Warrior (LHD #4)

The Dragon Family (LHD #5)

The Dragon's Discovery (LHD #6)

The Dragon's Pursuit (LHD #7)

The Dragon Collective / Cat & Lachlan (LHD #8 / TBD)

Love in Scotland

Crazy Scottish Love (LiS #1)

Chaotic Scottish Wedding (LiS #2)

Stonefire Dragons

Sacrificed to the Dragon (SD #1)

Seducing the Dragon (SD #2)

Revealing the Dragons (SD #3)

Healed by the Dragon (SD #4)

Reawakening the Dragon (SD #5)

Loved by the Dragon (SD #6)

Surrendering to the Dragon (SD #7)

Cured by the Dragon (SD #8)

Aiding the Dragon (SD #9)

Finding the Dragon (SD #10)

Craved by the Dragon (SD #11)

Persuading the Dragon (SD #12)

Treasured by the Dragon / Dawn & Blake (SD #13 / Sept 24, 2020)

Stonefire Dragons Shorts

Meeting the Humans (SDS #1)

The Dragon Camp (SDS #2)

The Dragon Play (SDS #3)

Stonefire Dragons Universe

Winning Skyhunter (SDU #1)

Transforming Snowridge (SDU #2)

Tahoe Dragon Mates

The Dragon's Choice (TDM #1)

The Dragon's Need (TDM #2)

The Dragon's Bidder / (TDM #3)

The Dragon's Charge / Brad & Tasha (TDM #4 / Nov 12, 2020)

The Dragon's Weakness / David & Tiffany (TDM #5 / Jan 14, 2021)

About the Author

Jessie Donovan has sold over half a million books, has given away hundreds of thousands more to readers for free, and has even hit the *NY Times* and *USA Today* best-seller lists. She is best known for her dragon-shifter series, but also writes about magic users, aliens, and even has a crazy romantic comedy series set in Scotland. When not reading a book, attempting to tame her yard, or traipsing around some foreign country on a shoestring, she can often be found interacting with her readers on Facebook. She lives near Seattle, where, yes, it rains a lot but it also makes everything green.

Visit her website at: www.JessieDonovan.com

Printed in Great Britain
by Amazon